Spirit
Lake

Tamarria Denga

To –
All my love and
the best Wk

ISBN-10: 0692108297
ISBN-13: 978-0692108291

Any references to historical events, real people, or real places are used fictitiously. Names, characters, and places are products of the author's imagination.

Front cover design by Vila Design.
Book design by Deborah Kabwang.

T.D. Writes Publishing
TDwrites@tamarriadenga.com
www.tamarriadenga.com

Scripture references were taken from the Holy Bible, New International Version®, NIV® Copyright ©1973, 1978, 1984, 2011 by Biblica, Inc.® Used by permission. All rights reserved worldwide.

DEDICATION

To my Lord and Savior, Jesus Christ…it really happened. Thank You. You are everything to me. I love you.

To my husband, Miguel…thank you for your endless support and determination in seeing that my dreams come true. I love you.

To my children, Angel, David, and Michael…thank you for being my motivation. I hope you'll always know that if mommy can do it, then so can you. I love you.

ACKNOWLEDGMENTS

My heart is filled with gratitude toward everyone who has inspired, supported, or helped me to bring this long awaited dream to fruition. First, I can't thank You enough, Lord. You are the reason I live, move, and have my being. I am more than aware that the art of storytelling is a gift from You, and I will forever use it for Your glory.

To my loving husband, Miguel, who has supported me in more ways than one; I am so thankful that the Lord has gifted me with you. Here's to 120.

Deborah, you are a godsend. I can't imagine how I would have gotten this novel done without you. You've been like a writer's guardian angel. Thank you for all that you've done.

Madeline, my editor, I have a newfound respect for editors because of you. After adding your special touch, I fell deeper in love with Spirit Lake. Thank you so much. There will be more novels to come, so I will be in touch.

Destiny, thank you for reading the first four chapters, and then grilling and hounding me for the rest. Your enthusiasm for the storyline and characters gave me hope that others will find the same joy and excitement that you experienced. I hope that you will enjoy reading Spirit Lake in its entirety.

Tara, my best friend, thank you for your unending support, putting up with me when I interrupted our girls' trip to work on this novel, and your constant threats that it better end the way you want it to. Ha! Whether it does or not, I hope you'll love it either way.

My sister, Rochale, if you hadn't pulled me away from R.L. Stine books back in high school, and introduced me to Eric Jerome Dickey, I'd probably be writing young adult fiction right now! You've always been my reading inspiration. Thank you.

Mom, thank you for inspiring me to write since I was little. I still hold dear all of the poems you've written and passed on to me. I promise to publish them one day, under your name of course. I love you.

To my daddy who's no longer with us, thank you for telling me I could do anything I set my mind to. I'm doing it and I hope that you're proud. I love you always.

ONE

*T*eylor backed into the hallway until her spine hit the wall. She watched helplessly as a team of medical personnel rushed into the room she'd just been ordered out of. She knew they'd been trained to remain calm and focused in such circumstances but she could feel the panic in the air. She could see the urgency in their eyes. Teylor inhaled deeply and exhaled slowly to keep away the dizziness that was threatening to bring her to the floor. Her hands were trembling so badly she thought they'd fall off. She brought them to the wall and steadied herself. With dry eyes full of fear, all she could do was watch as the door closed.

For as long as she could remember, her mother had always been fond of the bottle, and the older Teylor became, the less she saw her mother sober. Life had been difficult growing up with an alcoholic single parent, but Teylor loved her mom just the same. Her mother was what most would call a "functioning alcoholic." She held a steady job, made sure the bills were paid and there was food in the fridge, but not much more. By the time Teylor started junior high, she was doing all of the cooking and cleaning.

After work, her mother would fall into her customary routine of asking about Teylor's day while pouring her first drink. Then she'd make sure her daughter did her homework while having a couple more; eventually she'd pass out with a bottle in her hand. After Teylor went away to college, her mom's drinking became worse, and she was hospitalized for the first time. Teylor knew what she had to do, and after her first semester ended, she moved back home to care for her mother. Determined that she would never become a college dropout, Teylor drove an hour to school each day and made the same journey back home when classes were over. As hard as it was, her mother was her priority. Teylor was all she had.

Eventually, her mom's liver and kidneys began to fail, and she became too sick to do anything. Teylor dedicated nearly every moment to seeing after her mom. It was a miracle she found the time to finish her last semester, a bittersweet accomplishment because her mother was too sick to attend the graduation ceremony.

Over the next few years, the hospital visits became more frequent, the stays longer. For the past two weeks, she'd been confined to the bed in the room Teylor was now watching as if her own life depended on it, because in a way, it did. What would she do without her mom? More than anything Teylor wanted her mother to get up out of that hospital bed, grab her by the hand, and in her familiar feisty tone say, "Let's get outta here, sugar. I've had 'bout enough of this place," but that was wishful thinking. Still Teylor hoped for a miracle and pleaded with the God of heaven and earth. "Please," she whispered to herself as she gripped a metal bar bolted to the wall. "Please let her live." She couldn't pace; she couldn't cry. All she could do was watch and wait.

Time seemed to move in slow motion as Teylor stayed slumped against the wall, frozen. After what felt like an eternity, the door opened. Teylor still didn't move. An older black man wearing blue scrubs and a white coat came her way. Everything else blurred, and she focused in on his expressive coal-black eyes. His eyes said it all. Her mother was gone.

Everything went quiet around Teylor. The man was speaking but she couldn't hear him. Her knees buckled but she didn't fall. She gripped the metal bar tighter. She tried to breathe but her lungs were on fire. She wanted to go to her mother and tried to push herself off the wall just as the double doors to the right of her swung open. Teylor turned her head and looked into familiar eyes, full of love and sympathy. Suddenly she wasn't alone anymore. She reached for him as her legs gave out. He ran toward her, and before she could hit the floor, she felt him catch her. Then everything went black.

~

The memories of that day flooded Teylor like a summer storm. It would be two years this winter since her mother took flight, and even though she had accepted the fact that her mom was gone, on some days, the pain still felt as real as the day it had happened. Teylor refused to let today be one of those days, so she wiped at the mist in her eyes and went back to preparing dinner.

It was a moderately cool June evening so Teylor had the top half of her Dutch door open to allow the breeze to pass through her kitchen. She glanced at the round wooden clock hanging on the oatmeal-colored wall. Five-thirty. Jamie would arrive in half an hour. She checked her uncooked dinner rolls to make sure they'd risen to her liking. They'd be going in the oven in another ten minutes. She then gathered the dinner plates, napkins, and silverware and carried them to the small outdoor dining table on the back porch.

She glanced toward the lake that flowed behind her cottage. The sun hung low in a painted blue sky, and the trees were dressed in an array of green, pink, purple, and yellow. All signs that spring was nearing the end of her performance and summer was taking the stage. Spirit Lake was located east of the small town that shared its name. Most of the residents lived in the town proper, but those, like herself, who preferred to live in a quieter setting chose to live across the lake, in the "high country" as it was sometimes called.

The streetcar provided access from the town to the lake and vice versa. But the quickest way to access her part of town was by boat, and because the lake was such a huge part of the town's recreation, many of the residents owned one.

The view from her backyard always took Teylor's breath away. On the opposite side of the lake, she could see the tall buildings in the center of town. An abundance of trees, some with a colorful array of blooming flowers, were spread about the landscape like a lush leafy blanket while mountains sat in the distance. It was a picturesque scene that often reminded Teylor of a beautiful painting. She felt like she spent more time on her back porch admiring the scenery, reading, or writing than she did inside of her house. She even slept on her porch swing some nights.

Whenever Arizona came to mind, most people pictured a cacti-laden desert, surrounded by rock-covered mountains with wild coyotes running amok in the blistering heat. But Spirit Lake lay in the northern part of the state, where junipers and pines filled the land and the mountains wore snowcaps year round. Each season made a beautiful attempt to outdo the last.

As Teylor was setting out the serving dishes, she heard the faint familiar sound of a motorboat racing across the water. Within minutes Jamie was docking his boat, walking along the small pier, and heading up the grass hill toward her cottage. In a simple black V-neck T-shirt, blue jeans, and black sneakers, he was a breath of fresh air. Seeing him lit her up like the Fourth of July. She ran out to greet him, jumping in his arms. Jamie hugged her tight and spun her around. She wrapped her arms around his neck and held on tight, her giggles echoing through the evening air. Since her mother's passing, few things made her smile, but he never disappointed. For Teylor, Jamie was joy wrapped in a human package.

After a few more mutual squeezes, he put her down, and with his famous dimpled smile, asked, "Miss me much?"

She playfully nudged him in the chest with her fist. "Not at all."

Jamie stumbled back, feigning injury while holding his chest. "Careful, woman. I just spent thirteen hours on a plane. I'm too tired and too sore to take even your weak punches right now," he said, laughing.

Teylor let out a gasp. "Weak," she shouted. "You better be glad I'm taking pity on you. Don't let this five-seven frame fool you. I can take every bit of your six-two to the ground, homeboy."

Jamie laughed, grabbed her by the hand, and headed for the back porch. "What'd you cook? I'm starving."

He sat down at the table, and Teylor took the chair across from him. He lifted the lids on the two serving dishes and a pleased smile graced his smooth, deep brown face. "Looks like you missed me after all."

"In your dreams," she teased, rolling her eyes.

"The fact that you made my favorite says otherwise, my dear Mahogany."

Mahogany. One of his many nicknames for her. An ode to her skin, eyes, and thick curly hair, all reddish-brown. His most common name for her was TJ, a combination of their first initials, given to them by mutual friends because of the time they spent together. It used to be that you would never see one without the other. Over seventeen years, things hadn't changed much. He called her by her given name when he was upset or they were discussing serious matters, but Mahogany...Mahogany was her favorite. In her eyes, it was a term of endearment. Her mother once told her that Jamie called her that when he thought she was looking exceptionally beautiful. Teylor wasn't sure how right her mother was, considering she and Jamie had only ever been friends. Best friends.

"Hellooo, Earth to TJ."

Jamie's deep, melodic voice snapped her out of her thoughts. "I'm sorry, did you say something?"

He chuckled. "Yes. You wanna bless the food or do you want me to do it?"

"You go ahead."

Jamie said grace and after they both said amen, he began loading spoonfuls of rice and shrimp onto Teylor's plate. "This looks great, T," he said as he doubled the portions for himself. She smiled and ate, relishing having her friend back.

"So," he said, taking a bite of food, "what've you been up to since I've been away?"

She shrugged and replied, "Same ole, same ole. Writing. Trying to meet deadlines. I just finished the article for that journal I was telling you about. We'll see how that goes."

"It's gonna go awesome, TJ. You're the best writer I know."

"And how many writers do you know?" she teased.

"Personally? Only one, but it doesn't matter. You're still the best." He smiled and gave her a wink. Teylor shook her head and laughed. "You're so biased."

"Maybe. What about your book? Any more progress?"

Teylor let out a deep sigh. "Not as much as I would like, but I guess I'll get there."

Jamie grew quiet and stared at her. "What's on your mind, Teylor? You've been thinking about your mom today?"

She raised her curious eyes to meet his, and he gave her a knowing smile. "Why do you say that?"

"I know you, TJ."

He sat back in his chair and inclined his head toward the back door. Teylor closed her eyes and hung her head when she realized what he was referring to. "Billie," she said with a sheepish smile, "she always gives me away."

Billie Holiday's *The Very Thought of You* was flowing through the house like a soft current. The only thing that had gone well with her mother's drinking was Lady Day. Teylor would fall asleep hearing Billie sing from her mother's classical trumpet horn record player and wake up to the same jazz tunes. Today she was missing her, and she'd decided to listen to the beautiful jazz singer while she cooked dinner for Jamie. During the excitement of his arrival, she'd forgotten to change the music.

Teylor placed her dinner napkin on the table and pushed her chair back. "I'll change it to something else."

Jamie reached an arm across the table and grabbed her hand, stopping her in her tracks. His friendly eyes warmed her. "It's fine, Teylor. If you're okay with it, then so am I."

A nervous smiled graced her face while she wrestled with whether or not to change the music. She opted for the latter and sat down to continue dinner. Taking a sip of water, she changed the subject.

"So tell me," she said with a forced grin, "how was Paris?"

He watched her with concern for a long moment before replying. "Beautiful."

Teylor's eyebrows furrowed at his short answer. "That's it? You go to Paris for the first time and all you can say is that it was beautiful?" she asked in sportive bewilderment. "We're talking Paris. In springtime. Tell me something!"

Jamie laughed and spooned more food into his mouth. He chewed slowly as a teasing response to her growing impatience. She chuckled and threw a dinner roll at him. He caught it and took a bite.

"This is some good food, TJ," he said, taking another bite. Teylor reached for the basket of dinner rolls to throw at him, but Jamie tossed up his hands in surrender and said, "Okay. Okay. No need to get violent. You need to work on your patience, woman." He wiped his mouth with his dinner napkin and shrugged.

"Paris was everything you'd expect it to be during spring. Beautiful. Romantic. Inspiring. And expensive as hell!"

They both burst with laughter. "I'm serious," he said. "If I'd have stayed another day, I was gonna be sleeping on the streets and begging for food in three languages." Teylor kept laughing.

"Yeah right," she replied between chuckles. "You're not hurting for money, Jamie."

"Maybe not, but we were out there doing the most."

Confusion settled on Teylor's face as her laughter dwindled, and when Jamie's smile faded, she knew he regretted making his last statement. She was afraid to ask, but curiosity was forcing her to face her fear.

"We? Did you make friends out there?"

After taking a long drink of his sweet tea, he assessed her as if he was contemplating how to answer her question. Jamie licked his lips and like a slow water leak, his response trickled from his lips. "Carrie went with me."

Teylor stilled for a brief moment and then relaxed, hoping he hadn't noticed, but of course he had. He noticed everything.

"What's wrong?"

She raised her eyebrows and shook her head while she picked at the food on her plate. "Nothing. I just thought...I thought you were going alone, that's all."

"Does it bother you that I didn't?"

She forced herself to look at him with a less than genuine smile. "No. I just had no idea she was going."

"It wasn't planned. I had a two-day layover in New York—remember, I told you that?— and she decided last minute to come along."

Jamie had met Carrie on a business trip to New York six months ago. Ebony skin, athletic build, long jet black hair, and an executive in her parents' very successful real estate firm, Jamie had been instantly smitten by the beauty. He'd made several trips back there since their first meeting, but Carrie had yet to make an appearance in Spirit Lake.

Teylor cleared her throat and said, "I guess that made things interesting," once again refusing to meet his eyes.

He stayed silent until she did. When her gaze finally met his, she found amusement in his eyes. "I know what you're trying to ask me, TJ. Why don't you just come right out and ask?"

She shrugged in phony confusion. "I was simply making a statement. I wasn't trying to ask you anything."

"Okay," he said, taking another sip of tea. "Just so we're clear, I'm not answering the question you're not trying to ask me until you come right out and ask."

Teylor rolled her eyes and gave in to the bait. "Did you sleep with her?" she asked plainly.

Jamie sat back in his chair and smiled. "No, sweets, I did not."

Her eyes squinted skeptically.

"I swear to you I didn't. You know how I feel about that. Never again. Not before marriage."

"It's been five years, Jamie. You can't make me believe that being alone in Paris with a beautiful woman wasn't enough temptation to kill you."

"First, there are over two million people in Paris, so we weren't alone. Second, we got separate rooms, and I'm sitting here talking to you—alive, might I add—so it looks like I survived."

"Oh come on, Jamie. You weren't the least bit tempted?"

He met her with a serious gaze. "I'm tempted every day, Teylor, but like we agreed five years ago, never again until I'm married."

Teylor saw the weighty look in his eyes and raised her glass in salute. "Here's to your excellent ability to exercise self-control."

He chuckled and raised his glass to meet hers in the air. "But for the grace of God."

After they both took a sip, he leaned forward and rested his elbows on the table. His face once again grew serious, and she knew that whatever he was about to say next was something she wasn't quite prepared for. He focused on her with intensity and her heart raced. She waited.

"Speaking of marriage…" He paused, unsure of how she would respond. He'd always been that way toward her—careful, wanting to preserve her feelings, but little did he know that nothing would be able to prevent the damage that his next sentence would do to her heart.

"I asked Carrie to marry me…and she said yes."

TWO

Teylor sat frozen, unable to speak, her mouth slightly agape. Even though no words escaped her lips, her heart was speaking a language of its own. Sorrow.

She didn't want to be so obviously affected by his announcement but she couldn't help herself. Inside she was falling apart. She hadn't noticed that she was squeezing her dinner napkin until she followed Jamie's gaze to her hand on the table. She quickly let go and swallowed the lump in her throat. In an effort to gather her thoughts, she took slow, even breaths.

Jamie was fixed on her every facial expression. He knew she wasn't happy for him, and she knew that wasn't the reaction he was hoping for.

"Say something, Teylor," he said softly.

She gave him a careless shrug, offered a tired "Congratulations," stood from the table, and hurried into the house.

Feeling nauseous, she stood over the kitchen sink, gripping the cool granite countertop to brace herself. Jamie followed her in and gently touched her arm.

"Teylor, what's this about? I thought you'd be happy for me."

She whipped herself around to face him. "Why would you think something like that?" she asked harshly. "How am I supposed to be happy you're marrying someone I've never even met after just six months? *You* hardly even know her. I thought you would at least talk to me first, Jamie!"

Jamie stalled, hanging his head and running his fingers through his short sable curls. "I'm sorry. I knew I was risking you being annoyed with me for not talking to you first, but it never crossed my mind that you'd be this upset," he said meeting her eyes again.

"Well, I guess you don't know me as well as you think you do."

He winced but remained silent. Teylor closed her eyes and drew in a deep breath. "Look," she said, "I'm sorry. We were having a nice dinner, and you caught me off guard, and I...I guess I overreacted."

He studied her for a short while, unsure what to make of her apology. He reached for her hand but she pulled away and walked toward the back door.

"So, Jameson, why don't we finish talking about this tomorrow? I have some deadlines to meet."

Teylor knew he wasn't going to buy that. She'd called him Jameson—something she never did unless she was angry. It hadn't been her intention to do so, but she couldn't help herself. She was furious. Nausea continued to sweep over her, and at this point, she had to be alone so she could grab hold of her emotions.

"You said you finished your article, which means you've already met your deadline. Don't lie to me, Teylor."

She remained quiet.

"Look, Teylor—"

"I really have some things to work on. My book, perhaps. So if you don't mind." She went to the back door and held it open for him. She saw his jaw tighten and the solemn look in his eyes. It hurt her to hurt him, but she was fuming inside, and she wasn't one hundred percent sure why. She'd never met Carrie, but Jamie was a good judge of character. She knew he'd never choose to marry anyone she or his family would not approve. But then why hadn't he brought Carrie to Spirit Lake before proposing? And then there was the fact that he'd made the decision without even speaking to her first—but then again she knew, without him saying so, that she was the first person he'd told, even before his parents. Besides, Jamie was a grown man who could make his own decisions without her two cents. Still, Teylor felt like she was dying inside. She should be happy for the person she loved most in the world, but there was no joy.

She glanced at him again and saw him watching her, that same painful look on his face. She lifted her chin, looked away, and opened the door wider. He slowly shook his head and brushed past her without uttering a sound. She opened her mouth to say something, apologize, but no words escaped her lips. Besides what would she say? What she'd been denying to herself for the past seventeen years? She could never tell him the secret that had been hidden in her heart since her first encounter with him. The secret truth she'd been unsure of until that very moment. The real reason why it pained her to hear that he was marrying another woman. It was simple. That woman wasn't her.

She closed the door and rested against it. A long moment passed before she heard the motor of the boat starting, and as she listened to him speeding away, pain forced the tears down her face.

~

Jameson Westbrook was the youngest child and only son of Edward and Gail Westbrook. A tall and extremely handsome man who loved God and the people around him, he was also the best friend that Teylor had ever had and the man she happened to be in love with—unbeknownst to him. A small-town boy with a huge heart, co-owner of a transportation brokerage company started by his father years ago, and newly engaged to a beautiful woman he'd met on a business trip.

Teylor could rip her own heart out if he wasn't already doing it for her. How could she have let this happen? She'd known Jamie was crazy about Carrie but she hadn't been aware that he'd completely lost his mind. The only man she'd ever loved was not only in love with someone else, but was also planning to make that someone else his wife.

Teylor lay in bed with a cool towel on her head and a heating pad on her stomach. After the night she'd just had, she felt like she was coming down with the flu. Maybe there really was such a thing as being lovesick. But what was the cure? She and Jamie had shared more than half their lives together; how could he not know that she was the one? First her mom had left her and soon Jamie would too.

Teylor pressed the cool towel to her forehead. Her head ached tremendously and she desperately needed some ibuprofen, but getting up proved to be more challenging than enduring the pain, so she stayed put. She tried not to cry because crying made everything worse, but holding back the tears was beginning to make her throat burn.

She grabbed her cell from her nightstand and pulled up one of her social media accounts. She entered a name in the search engine and browsed the thumbnails until she found what she was looking for.

Carrie King's profile picture was enough to make Teylor want to throw the phone across the room. She and Jamie stood locked in a kiss in front of a scenic view of the lower half of the Eiffel Tower.

Carrie's account was set to private, but Teylor was able to click on the picture and see the likes and comments. Over two hundred of each, all sending their congratulations and support to the beautiful couple. But not one name was familiar to her, and Teylor noticed that Carrie hadn't tagged Jamie in the picture. Still that made sense if he hadn't told his family yet.

Teylor placed her phone back on the nightstand. She'd seen enough. Her headache worsened so she forced herself into the kitchen to take medicine. It was going to be a long night.

~

Jamie was sprawled across his bed, face up and watching the ceiling. He glanced at the clock on the table to the left of him. Four a.m. Eyes back on the ceiling, he prayed for sleep, but thoughts of Teylor plagued him.

He thought back to her reaction after he'd told her about his engagement. Her anger still confused him, and racking his brain to solve that puzzle was depriving him of sleep. Maybe he should have spoken to her before he proposed, but it hadn't been his plan to ask Carrie to marry him. Being with her in Paris just felt right, and he saw himself building a life with her, having children, and traveling the world. Now he wondered how Teylor would fit into this new life—or if she even wanted to.

The thought of living his life without her danced on the surface of his mind, but he quickly drove it away. Jamie didn't have the strength to face the now possible reality the two of them might part ways, and he needed sleep more than anything.

He checked his phone for what seemed like the hundredth time since leaving Teylor's house. Eight missed calls and five text messages, but nothing from her. Carrie had called twice but he knew he'd be forced to tell her the reason for his melancholy tone, and he didn't want her getting a bad impression of his best friend whom he'd spoken so highly of. He wanted two of the most important women in his life to be like sisters—assuming Teylor wanted to continue being in his life at all.

The rest were from his friend and co-worker Saber, who unquestionably wanted to talk about work and how many French girls he'd met while in Paris; his mother, who he knew was checking to make sure he'd made it back safe; and his sister, Charleston, who more than likely was being harassed by their mom to make sure she'd called and checked that he'd returned in one piece. He reminded himself to call his mom first thing after he got some sleep, but everyone else would have to wait.

Jamie continued to watch the ceiling and thought of his best friend. He was grateful an hour later, when sleep finally found him.

~

Jamie pulled up to his parents' two-story colonial later that morning. His sister, Charleston, had been housesitting for the past week while his parents were visiting family in Texas. He'd spoken to his mother shortly before arriving, but hadn't had the energy to tell her about the engagement. Trying to figure out whatever was really plaguing Teylor was taking what strength he had left. His parents would be home in a few days, then he'd be able to talk to them and get sound advice.

Jamie found Charleston in the sunlit breakfast nook eating pecan pancakes. The kitchen door was open, and he heard his niece and nephew playing in the backyard. Charleston stood and greeted him with a smile and a warm hug.

"Hey, lil bro, glad you made it back safe. Grab a plate, pull up a chair, and tell me all about Paris," she ordered as she sat back down.

"Gotta say 'what's up' to the rug rats first," he said and exited through the screen door.

After hugging, kissing, and answering what seemed like a hundred questions from his overly excited niece and nephew, Jamie headed back inside to talk to Charleston.

"I missed those kiddos," he said, grabbing her juice to take a sip. Without missing a beat, she snatched the cup away just before it touched his lips.

"Get your own. Plenty in the fridge," she said, pointing toward the stainless steel icebox.

"So selfish," he said with a smirk.

"Whatever. Anyway, they missed you too. Asked me every day when you were coming home. I had to mark the date with a big red circle on the calendar in the kitchen so they would leave me alone."

He grinned from ear to ear, and Charleston playfully rolled her eyes. She went to the stove and loaded a plate with pancakes and turkey bacon and placed it on the table in front of him.

"So, Paris. Tell me all about it."

Jamie sighed and ran his hands through his thick hair, tilting his head to rest on the chair's wooden back. He was already so tired of talking about Paris that the mere mention of anything French made him want to pull his curls out. He fought to erase the events of the previous night, but lost that battle as he found himself once again watching the ceiling.

"Jamie."

Jamie popped his head up and met his sister's worried eyes. She'd stopped eating and turned his way.

"Yeah?"

"What's wrong?"

Jamie slumped in his chair. "I'm functioning on three hours of sleep. I'm tired."

Charleston sucked her teeth. "I've seen you run a half marathon on less sleep than that. Come on now, you know I know you better than that."

"Yeah well, you think you know someone..." His voice trailed off as his eyes shot back to the ceiling.

"Are you going to find sleep looking up at the ceiling?" she cracked. When he didn't laugh, her tone turned serious.

"Baby bro, talk to me. Your entire mood changed when I asked about Paris. What happened?"

Jamie took a deep breath and sat up straight in his chair. He studied his sister's worried face, which so resembled their mother's. Her dark, almond-shaped eyes watched him with intensity, and he noticed a touch of sadness in them that he knew had nothing to do with him. Her unruly chocolate-colored curls were tied in a bun at the crown of her head, and he couldn't remember the last time he'd seen her with her hair down. Something else was definitely troubling his sister, and he made a mental note to ask her about it later.

But first he had to tell her. He took a deep breath. "I asked Carrie to marry me," he said finally.

Charleston's eyes widened, and her mouth fell open. "You did what?!"

"You heard me," he said plainly.

Charleston responded with a long drawn out, "Okaaaaaay." Then she tilted her head in confusion. "So why the gloomy mood? Did she say no?"

"Nope."

"So I'm assuming she said yes?"

"Yep."

Charleston shook her head, baffled. "What am I missing? Aren't you supposed to be excited? I mean you keep staring up at the ceiling but you're not exactly jumping to the moon."

"I was at first, but…"

"But what?"

Jamie hesitated.

"But what, little bro?"

"I told Teylor, and she flipped out on me." Seeing the confused look on Charleston's face, he elaborated. "She got mad. Asked me how I could do this without consulting her first, and then she practically threw me out of her house."

Nodding her head slowly, Charleston said, "I see."

"You see what? You know something I don't?"

"Like what?"

"Like why she's upset?" Charleston chuckled and picked up her fork to jab at her pancakes. Jamie grabbed the fork and placed it back on the table. "Please, Charlie," he pleaded. "I need to fix this. I don't know what I did, and it's frustrating the hell outta me."

Charleston sighed and turned back to her brother. "Look, Jamie, it's not your fault. Teylor is just reacting the way any woman in her shoes would."

"Meaning?"

"Meaning, she's scared she's losing her best friend."

A frown covered his face. "That's ridiculous."

"Is it? Think about it, Jamie, how many male friends have you seen me hanging with since I've been married? Or Mom, for that matter? Have you ever seen Dad kickin' it with any female buddies?" He didn't answer. "Exactly."

Her voice grew quiet. "Listen, Jamie, since the eighth grade you two have been inseparable. You've shared more than half of your lives together as best friends. You've been the most important person in her life, and she's been the most important person in yours. Everybody knows that. But now that you're getting married, she's not sure where she's going to fit in…if at all. For all she knows, she's kicked to the curb like Thursday's trash."

Jamie winced at the analogy. "I would never do that to her," he said softer than he'd intended.

"Yeah well, you may not want to but once you're married, your 'I' becomes 'we.' It's not only up to you. Life is about to change, little brother."

She took one last bite then sauntered to the sink to wash her dish. Jamie sat and thought for a long moment. Charleston made a good point, but Teylor knew him better than that. They'd both been in serious relationships in the past and still managed to maintain their friendship. They always made time for each other, and their relationship outlasted all of the others they'd had. Why should this be any different? Carrie was a secure and understanding woman. She wouldn't feel threatened or intimidated by his and Teylor's friendship. That, Jamie was sure of. She'd be his wife, and Teylor would always remain his best friend.

~

After drying and putting away her plate, Charleston walked over to the back door and silently watched her children play. Neither of them said another word and after a while, Jamie kissed her on the cheek, left the kitchen, and walked out the front door. Charleston was concerned for him. She knew he was more upset than he'd let on. If there was one thing she knew for sure, it was that Jamie's favorite breakfast food was pecan pancakes. She turned and glanced at his untouched plate. "You'll figure it out, little brother," she said aloud to herself and continued watching her children play.

THREE

Saber stood at the front desk of S.L. Enterprises sweet-talking Cassie. His tall, muscular six-three frame towered over the receptionist's desk but he was bent low, their faces only about six inches apart. The brunette was giddy with excitement as Saber whispered in her ear.

"I always see you checking me out," he said in a deep melodic tone.

"What makes you think that?" she asked, her voice light and sultry.

"Oh, so you don't?"

"I didn't say that," she responded. "I just wanted to know what made you think I was."

He traced her jawline with his finger. "It's a yes or no question, sweetheart." He pierced her brown eyes with his emerald gaze.

"Your eyes are so beautiful," she responded. "And I love your red hair," she continued as she fingered his beard.

He smiled and took her hand in his. "I can make you love some other things about me," he said softly.

"Like what? The fact that she's probably the third woman you've fed that line to today?"

Saber grinned and turned toward the familiar voice. Jamie was standing there with an equally large smile plastered across his face.

"My man," Saber said smoothly, and they exchanged a handshake and brotherly hug. "Glad you made it back safe, man. Finally decided to show your face at the office, I see."

"Yeah, I figured you all might've missed me around here. And it looks like I came just in time." Jamie gave a nod in Cassie's direction.

"Good morning, Cassie."

She smiled sheepishly, said, "Morning, Jamie, welcome back," and quickly directed her attention to her computer screen.

Saber chuckled, glanced at Cassie, and said, "I've been handling things just fine around here." He winked at her, making her turn beet red.

Jamie shook his head and led the way to his office.

Once he and Saber were inside, Jamie said, "Do you have to mess around with the women who work for us, Sabe? We're trying to run an upstanding company."

"And you do a fantastic job at it, bro."

Jamie took a seat behind his desk in his black leather office chair, and Saber sat down opposite him.

"Saber, I'm serious."

"So am I. You're the saint. I've never claimed to be. You represent this company and you do it well. I know your dad's proud," he responded sarcastically.

Jamie cocked his head and stared down his friend. Saber threw up his hands in defense.

"No offense, Jamie. I'm just saying, you know this is me. It's always been me, and it will always be me. I love women. Period. Don't act brand new."

"Well, I'm just saying," Jamie replied boldly, "exercise some self-control, especially in the workplace."

20

They had a stare down for a short moment until Saber gave Jamie a cool nod. "Whatever you say, boss."

After another brief moment of silence, they both erupted in laughter.

"Man, you need help," Jamie said, chuckling.

"That's what they keep telling me," Saber quipped.

"Anyway, on to the juicy details," Saber said, rubbing his hands together. "Let's talk about—"

Jamie quickly threw his hand up. "Before you even go there. I. Am. Not. Talking. About. Paris."

A disappointed countenance washed over Saber. "What?!"

Jamie shook his head. "Not doing it."

"Come on, man, you can't leave me hanging. I need to know something."

"Something," Jamie responded casually and started going through his emails.

Saber let out a wounded chuckle. "Okay, okay. You got jokes. You're not funny, but you got jokes."

Jamie sat with amusement etched on his face. "And furthermore, I'm glad that you find this to be entertaining. Leaving your boy hanging out to dry. What kind of friend are you?"

Jamie was full-on laughing by this time. He was thankful for Saber's sense of humor. This was the first time he'd really laughed since his fight with Teylor.

"Alright, man. In Paris…"

Saber rolled his hands, gesturing for Jamie to come on out with it.

"In Paris, I got engaged."

Saber's eyes widened, and he almost fell out of his chair. Jamie rolled his eyes at his friend's dramatic reaction.

After Saber finally gathered himself together, he said, "You mean to tell me, you went to Paris, the city of Love, with all those French honeys, and actually fell in love? And asked one of them to marry you! After two weeks! Maaaaan, get out of here! You're pulling my leg, right?"

Jamie sat quietly with a straight face. When he saw that Jamie was being sincere, Saber had to take a moment to gather himself, after almost falling out of his chair once again.

He then got up, left Jamie's office, came back with a cup of coffee, sat back down, and said, "Explain."

Jamie went over everything that had happened over the past few days. The engagement, Teylor's reaction, and Charleston's explanation. When he was done, Saber sat there slowly shaking his head with his mouth open in shock.

"I believe that for the first time in my life, I am at a loss for words."

Jamie nodded in agreement. "I hear ya, man."

"So what now?"

Jamie shrugged. "I get married, I guess."

"You're sure about this?"

"I believe so. Yeah."

"You don't sound convinced."

"It's not that, I just can't figure out what's up with Teylor, and it's about to drive me crazy."

Saber let out a deep sigh. "Well, don't you two still meet up at Lucy's every week?"

"Yeah."

"So get her to talk to you. Maybe she's had time to cool down."

"Yeah, but she hasn't answered any of my calls or texts. I'm not even sure she'll show up."

"She'll show."

"How can you be so sure?"

"Women are funny like that, man. I've been with enough to know that I haven't quite figured them out yet, but I've been able to decipher a few of their codes. Don't worry, she'll be there."

Jamie stared off into space and rubbed his goatee. "I hope so."

"I'll tell you what," Saber quipped. "It couldn't be me. That's why I always tell you not to put all of your eggs into one basket. Then you went and threw the whole damn basket away! Have I not taught you anything?"

Jamie laughed and shook his head at him.

"One honey. How can a man deprive himself of all the gorgeous women out there just to be devoted to one?" Saber shook his head. "Not happening."

"And I don't get how a man can dive into everything he sees walking," Jamie fired back.

"Now I resent that," Saber said, raising a finger. "I don't dive into everything. The booty has to be fat...and then I dive."

They both erupted in laughter.

~

A few days went by, and Jamie still hadn't heard from Teylor. His calls and texts went unanswered. Today they were supposed to meet at Lucy's for their weekly lunch date, and he wasn't sure she'd be there. Still hopeful, he sent one last text.

Heading to Lucy's. We really need to talk.

He waited ten minutes, and with no response, headed out the door. He decided that enough was enough. If Teylor didn't show up for lunch, he was making his way across the lake.

~

Teylor entered Lucy's ten minutes late for her lunch date with Jamie. The small diner was moderately crowded with the same familiar faces that made the eatery their routine lunch choice. There were black booths aligned along the windows on the left side of the diner, a bar to the right, and white free-standing tables with matching chairs in the center. The walls were painted a soft mint green and graced with old black and white photos of Spirit Lake through the ages.

Teylor didn't have to scan the room to find Jamie. He was sitting with his back to her in their regular booth that looked out at the bookstore across the street. Years before Teylor had chosen that booth specifically for that purpose. She loved the bookstore and enjoyed seeing patrons going excitedly to and fro with new and used books in hand.

Teylor nodded and smiled at acquaintances as she made her way to Jamie. He was busy with his phone when she sat down in the seat opposite him. His eyes stretched when he looked up and saw her.

"Hello," she said in a formal tone.

"Hey, Teylor, I'm glad you made it." He paused. "I wasn't sure you would."

"Why not? Every week like clockwork."

She took a sip of the sweet iced tea he'd ordered for her. He looked at her, not needing to state the obvious. Of course he had every right to doubt that she would make their weekly lunch date. She hadn't spoken to him since their last encounter and knew he wondered if she would ever speak to him again, but as much as she'd like to play hardball, Teylor couldn't deny what was in her heart, and living her life without Jamie seemed next to impossible.

Sandy, Lucy's twenty-two-year-old granddaughter and their regular waitress, came bouncing over with a plate in each hand. She wore her normal uniform—black tee, black jeans, and a white and black checkered waist apron. Her big brown eyes lit up like lightbulbs when she saw Teylor had arrived.

"Hey, Teylor," she said excitedly.

Teylor smiled genuinely in response as Sandy placed Jamie's plate in front of him. "I'll go ahead and start your order since you're here. Jamie guessed southwest chicken salad, dressing on the side, was he right?" Teylor nodded. "Oh, and this is for you," Sandy said, setting a small plate of biscuits with strawberry preserves in front of her. "He also said if I saw you come in, I shouldn't approach the table without your favorite."

Teylor looked at Jamie, and his eyes met hers. He knew her so well. She usually chose between four or five entrees on the menu, but she always ordered a side of biscuits with strawberry preserves. He also knew that the southwest chicken salad was one of her favorites, and it made her wonder. How could the man who knew her better than anyone else in the world not know that she was in love with him? Couldn't he see it in the way she looked at him? Every time their eyes met it was like electricity flowed through her. Could he not feel it? How could he not know that of all the men she'd ever dated, he, her best friend, was the one who had her heart? And most of all, how could he give his to another woman?

Jamie interrupted her thoughts. "Sandy, I ordered potato salad, not French fries."

"Oh, that's right. I'm so sorry, Jamie. You normally get the hand-cut fries so I got mixed up. I'll get it fixed for you. You can keep the French fries if you like. No charge."

He quickly hid his grimace with a smile. Sandy didn't notice but Teylor did. Sandy turned her attention back to Teylor. "Girl, you were late today," she said with her hands on her hips. "You're usually the first one here. I thought you were standing my homie up." She giggled.

Sandy was kind although blunt, always speaking without thinking but never intending harm to anyone. She was a lot like her grandmother Lucy in that way.

Teylor offered a sheepish smile. "No, don't think I'd have the heart to do that."

Her eyes met Jamie's once again. Sandy grew quiet and cleared her throat. "Well, I'll leave y'all to it. Jamie, I'll be right back with that side of potato salad." She rushed off and disappeared into the kitchen.

"You don't like fries anymore?" Teylor asked.

"Yeah, I'm just not too fond of anything that has the word 'French' attached to it these days."

Sandy came hurrying back over with the potato salad and Teylor's salad. "My apologies again, Jamie. Here you are, Teylor," she said as she placed Teylor's plate in front of her. "Y'all enjoy your meal now," and she was off again.

Teylor forked some salad, but before she could put it in her mouth, Jamie called her name, stopping her. He stared at her, and she set the fork down.

"Go ahead."

After he finished saying grace, they sat in silence and ate.

Teylor sensed Jamie's eyes on her off and on, but he remained quiet until they were halfway through their meal.

"Do you wanna talk about what happened?"

"Not really," she answered, still eating and not looking up at him.

"Okay. Is this friendship over then?"

She sat down the biscuit that she was nibbling on and looked him in the eye. "You tell me."

"What's that supposed to mean? You kick me out of your house and then—"

"I did not kick you out of my house, Jamie."

"Well, what would you call it?"

"I simply deescalated the situation by suggesting that you leave."

Jamie chuckled and shook his head. "Okay, we'll play your game. You—"

"I'm not playing games," she interjected again.

Jamie closed his eyes, took a deep breath, and rested his forehead on his clasped hands. He was an extremely patient man but even she could see that he was getting frustrated with her. He opened his eyes and engaged her once again; this time his voice was calm.

"Okay, Teylor, just talk to me. Tell me whatever it is that's on your mind. Don't hold back."

She fought with her emotions. She wanted to come right out and say it then. Scream it amidst the townspeople. Pour her heart out for all to hear. *I'm in love with you! Can't you see it?* But she couldn't. The risk could cost her the only person she found hard to live without.

Instead, she looked away and said, "You wouldn't understand."

"Then make me understand," he retorted through clenched teeth.

He was angry, but she knew it wasn't aimed at her; he simply didn't understand why his most cherished relationship was falling apart right before his eyes and more than that, he didn't know how to stop it. Jamie took a deep breath and tried to calm down. He took her hands in his, and she left them there a moment, savoring his touch. Then she gently pulled them away. When she met his gaze again, his pain was evident. It was tearing her apart, and she couldn't keep doing this to him.

She glanced out of the window at the bookstore. There was a couple making their way inside hand in hand, drowning in love and happy endings. Maybe that would never be her and Jamie, and as much as that possibility pierced her to her very core, she'd rather have him in her life as a friend than nothing at all. She exhaled and turned toward him.

"Jamie, forgive me," she said softly.

His dark eyes pierced hers. They held a hint of skepticism. He was unsure of her sudden change of heart. His mouth opened to speak but he didn't say anything, so she continued. "I don't want to lose you." Tears formed in the corners of her eyes, and her voice quaked. "You've been the most important person in my life and I…I'm scared."

"Of what?"

"Of not being the most important person in yours," she admitted.

Embarrassed, Teylor covered her face with her hands. "I know, this is so selfish of me."

Jamie gently pulled her hands from her face. Her tear-filled eyes met his caring gaze. "No, not selfish. Just honest."

He brushed a curl from her face with his forefinger and wiped her tears. His loving gesture made her want to burst into uncontrollable sobs. He was always so mindful of her feelings, protective even. Why couldn't he be hers forever? In order to keep things from getting more complicated, she gained control of her emotions and offered up a warm smile instead.

~

Jaime smiled back, but wondered if her worries were justified. He couldn't deny it, Teylor *was* the most important person in his life, even above all close friends and relatives, his parents and Charleston included. He had love for her that was indescribable. It was more than a friend's or sibling's love, different from a lover's. It was as if she'd become a part of him over the years. He was sure he loved Carrie, but the thought of his and Teylor's relationship changing weighed on his soul. He wanted to offer her some sort of reassurance but he didn't want to make promises he wasn't sure he could keep. The only promise he felt confident in was the one he gave.

"I'll always love you, Teylor."

FOUR

"**G**irl, whatcha got to eat in here?"
Rima was bent over rummaging through the fridge in Teylor's kitchen.

"Whatever you can find is yours, greedy."

Rima popped her head above the refrigerator door and gave her friend the evil eye. Her fire-red dreadlocks framed her face in spiral curls, and her honey brown eyes squinted with resentment. "I beg your pardon," Rima responded jokingly.

Teylor chuckled, and Rima went back to scavenging.

"How's the café? I haven't been in for about a week."

Rima opened the lid of a large Tupperware bowl and smiled when she saw yesterday's lasagna. "Yeah, I've noticed."

She grabbed a plate from the cabinet and helped herself to a big portion.

"The café's doing great. Same as usual," she said, walking through the kitchen door and taking a seat at the table on the back porch.

Teylor, chai tea in hand, followed her and sat on the porch swing. The day was warm and the sun was bright—its rays cast a shimmering reflection on the lake, giving it the appearance of a diamond-studded sea. The sight, along with the pungent aroma of freshly cut grass, made Teylor smile.

"Don't forget I have my showcase in a couple of weeks; you promised to read a poem, girl. Remember?"

Rima owned a small café in town and on the weekends after dark, it turned into a jazz club. Singers and musicians from all over Arizona performed on Saturday nights, and in two weeks, Rima herself would be the featured artist. Her soulful voice was beautiful, and Teylor was excited to see her friend's first official concert.

"You know I wouldn't miss it," Teylor responded. "And I already have a poem in mind."

Rima's huge smile showed her appreciation, and then she changed the subject. "Girl, why do you always cook so much food?" she asked, taking another bite of the lasagna.

Teylor shrugged and sipped her tea.

"Still used to cooking for Jamie, huh?"

Teylor took another sip of chai and said nothing. She stared out at the lake and focused on a group of teenagers swimming and laughing, no cares at all. Jamie and Carrie came to mind, and she forced herself to think of something else. The last thing she needed was to break down in front of Rima.

"Speaking of Jamie," Rima said, interrupting her thoughts. "He came into the café yesterday and told me he's getting married." She stopped eating and stared at Teylor.

Teylor kept her eyes on the laughing teenagers and quietly said, "I know." She and Jamie had spent countless hours during their teen summers swimming and boating in Spirit Lake. Later, Rima and Saber would often tag along, but it was always special when it was just the two of them.

"And?"

"And what, Rima?" Teylor asked, finally turning to look at her.

"How are you holding up? And don't say fine because I can look at you and see that you're not."

Teylor stared down at her cup and shrugged. "How should I be doing?" she asked. "I'm happy for him."

"Lies," Rima countered boldly.

"It's not a lie. I want whatever he wants. He's my best friend. Why wouldn't I be happy for him?"

Rima hesitated before responding and then let the words roll off her tongue. "Because you're in love with him," she said plainly.

Teylor nearly spit out the tea she'd just sipped. She shot Rima a surprised look. "Wh—what?"

Rima stood from the table and walked over to the swing to take a seat beside her. "Girl, who are you kidding," she said, staring Teylor in the eye. "I've known you since college. I can see it in your face when you hear his name, not to mention the way you look at him. Now, if you're going to lie to me, at least give me the respect and not look me in my eye and do it."

Teylor's bottom lip tightened and she looked away. As much as she wanted to lie through her teeth and deny her feelings for Jamie, she couldn't.

"Humph," Rima sighed and looked out at the lake. She watched the same teens that Teylor had been admiring frolicking about, and Teylor knew she was having her own flashbacks of previous times. Happier times.

"Remember how we used to swim in the lake summer nights?"

Teylor smiled and nodded.

"My parents would get so upset because I would never leave Arizona right after school ended for break." She let her head fall back to rest on the porch swing. "I always spent a few days here first. This place just felt like home from the first moment you invited me here. I guess that's why I never went back to Louisiana after graduation."

Rima was originally from Baton Rouge. The only child of two loving but divorced parents, she'd come to Arizona for college and been Teylor's roommate in the dorm. They'd been friends ever since. Even when Teylor had to move back home after her first semester, she and Rima remained close. The fact that Rima had left Baton

Rouge so soon after high school and always found excuses not to go back home plagued Teylor, but she didn't want to pry so she'd never asked. She just kept inviting her friend to Spirit Lake until Rima moved there herself, after a brief stint at a big company in Phoenix. Even though she seemed content with her life, Teylor could still see a sadness that lingered behind her friend's beautiful hazel eyes.

They'd been sitting quiet for a moment when Rima finally asked, "Why don't you tell him?"

Teylor sucked her teeth. "And say what? 'Congratulations on your marriage and by the way, I'm in love with you'? We've been best friends since eighth grade, Rima. He probably looks at me like a little sister. I can't bear to lose him as a friend."

Rima turned to face her. Her tone was sterner than before. "You're going to lose him anyway, T. He's getting married. Do you know what that means? She comes first. There won't be any more late-night dinners under the stars, or three-hour phone conversations. No more sleeping at each other's houses to watch those corny eighties movies y'all love so much. No more boat rides on the lake. Nothing. It'll all change once the 'I do's' are spoken."

Rima sat back and continued swinging. As they both swayed back and forth, Teylor no longer had the strength to hide her emotions, and like she'd so often been doing since she'd learned of Jamie's engagement, she cried. The tears seemed endless. Rima wrapped her arm around her and brought her head to her shoulder.

"It's alright, girl. Get it all out."

She waited a moment and listened as Teylor drained her heart's pain in sobs. Finally, through her own tears, Rima said, "You and Jamie have what most people only dream about. I've always admired that about you two. If you tell him, T, and he denies you, it will hurt like hell. I won't lie to you about that, but eventually, through prayer and support from those who love you, you will get through it and move on. But if you don't say anything, you will never forgive yourself for not allowing yourself the opportunity to at least know what might've happened."

And with that said, they continued to swing while the tears flowed and the sun set.

~

The text read, *Meet me in the middle.*

A chill accompanied the evening so Teylor grabbed a light jacket and headed to her boat. "Meet me in the middle" was a code phrase she and Jamie used when either of them wanted the other to meet them halfway, in the middle of the lake. They'd shut their motorboats off, tie them together, and talk on the water. Sometimes for hours.

Teylor heard Jamie's boat before she started hers, and by the time she reached the lake's center, he was waiting for her. Jamie did the tying while Teylor admired the stars. They were especially bright tonight. The moon was high, the sky was clear, and the night silent. The quiet was one of the reasons Teylor had moved to the high country in the first place. It was perfect for writing.

"So how are you?" Jamie asked, bringing her attention back to him. She knew he wanted to make sure that everything was still good between them.

"I'm good, Jamie." He nodded slowly, seeming content with her answer.

"What made you want to meet in the middle tonight?" she asked.

"Do I always have to have a reason?" He shrugged. "Just felt like it, I guess."

Teylor raised a skeptical eyebrow, and he chuckled. She smiled. Seeing his dimples always had that effect on her.

"Okay," he confessed, "I just wanted to make sure that *we're* okay."

His eyes mimicked dark jewels beneath the night sky. The way he stared at her, with so much love, made her want to tell him everything right then and there, in the middle, under a bejeweled sky. Instead, she responded with a simple, "We are."

"Are you sure?"

"I am."

He smirked. "Why are you looking at me like that?"

She frowned in confusion, unaware that she'd been looking at him in any particular way.

"Like what?"

Jamie shook his head. "Never mind."

He directed his attention toward the sky, and Teylor was glad he'd let it go. The last thing she wanted was to be caught looking at him like a lovesick puppy.

Silence settled in, and they both took in their surroundings. She wondered what was on his mind, if he was sure he was making the right decision. No one had even met Carrie, yet he was intent on making her his wife. There Teylor sat right in front of him, and he'd never once considered that she'd make a better match for him. The thought threatened to bring her to tears, so she forced it out of her mind.

"Are you scared, Jamie?"

His eyes found hers again. "Of what?"

"Getting married."

Jamie let out a heavy sigh. "No, not of marriage."

"Of something else then?"

Jamie paused before giving his answer. "Of losing all of this." He gestured with his hands at their surroundings.

"You can be married and live in Spirit Lake, Jamie."

"I was talking about us, Teylor. This…everything we do together, what we've been doing since we were kids. It's hard to think that it could all change just because one of us decides to get married."

"Then don't get married," she countered boldly.

His laugh pierced the night.

"And then what, Teylor? We'll just be single forever with the promise of remaining best friends?"

Or you can marry me, was what she really wanted to say. Instead, she remained quiet.

"I don't know," Jamie said with a shrug, "what if the three of us become best friends?"

34

The skeptical eyebrow raise reappeared on Teylor's face.

"Seriously, what if you two hit it off so well that she replaces me as your best friend?"

"No one could replace you, Jamie."

Teylor spoke before realizing what she'd said. His gaze told her that it meant something, but he didn't allow it to leave his thoughts and travel from his lips. She was tinged with embarrassment but didn't try and rectify it. She meant every word.

"What if it were me?" she asked. "What if I were the one getting married? How would you feel?"

"Women are different, T. They handle things differently."

"Okay, I'll give you that, but only because men have too much ego to admit how they truly feel."

"You might have a point," he admitted.

"Okay, so pride aside...how would you feel?"

Jamie cocked his head as he contemplated how to answer. "Truthfully, I don't know, TJ."

"Why not?"

"I guess I'd have to be in that situation to know for sure."

"Truthful enough," Teylor said. "I guess one never knows how they will react until they are faced with something. I certainly didn't expect to react the way I did."

Jamie nodded slowly. "I think it's safe to say we were both surprised."

Teylor shifted in the boat. The real reason she'd become so upset at the announcement would set off a whole new chain of events, and he was looking at her as if he knew the truth.

"Relax, T. We don't have to go there again."

He had the ability to read her like a book, something she adored and hated about their relationship. He knew when she needed him without her having to say a word, and he knew things she wanted to keep hidden from him, which made her wonder—did he know that she was in love with him?

"Are you going to be my best girl?"

Teylor's face scrunched up. "Huh?"

"In the wedding. You're not a man so you can't be the best man. You'll be my best girl."

Teylor laughed out loud. "That's crazy, Jamie. Ask Saber."

"Saber's not my best friend. You are."

I'd rather be the bride.

"The bride is your best girl. That's why you're marrying her."

"I take it that's a no?"

"I'll support you in whatever way I can, Jamie. Your happiness is everything. You know that."

Jamie smiled and slowly stood in the boat, steadying himself by holding on to the edge. He leaned over and kissed her on the cheek.

"Go home and get some sleep. I'll wait until you make it inside before I take off."

He loosened the ropes that held their boats together, and Teylor hoped it wasn't a bad omen of what was to come—letting her go.

"Good night, Jamie."

"Good night, Mahogany."

~

The call came at seven Sunday morning while Jamie was getting out of bed to get ready for church. He dressed hurriedly and dashed out of the house, doing eighty-five on the interstate. He wasn't sure how he was supposed to feel—excited or worried. He'd just patched things up with Teylor, but her reaction to this new development was about to change things again—that he was sure of.

He tried calling her three times. No answer. Leaving a message was not an option. Neither was a text. He didn't want her to find out that way. Maybe he was being paranoid and things would go better than he thought. A man was allowed to hope, right? He recalled their conversation at Lucy's. She wanted to remain the most important person in his life. How was he supposed to make that happen when he was engaged to someone else? It was impossible. The last thing Jamie wanted to do was hurt Teylor, and now he was about to bring her face-to-face with her misery. She had apologized and said that things were okay between them, but he was still skeptical. Her reaction to the news was much more than what she said it was—he could feel it—but until she was completely honest with him, there was nothing he could do about it. As much as he could control it, she would always remain his best friend.

An hour and forty-five minutes later, Jamie entered Phoenix. He raced down Interstate 17 and hopped on the ramp that led to I-10. He silently thanked God that there was no traffic. He had ten minutes to make it to his destination.

He pulled up just in time, knowing it was waiting for him—either peace or chaos. He prayed it was the former.

FIVE

S unday morning found Teylor sifting through her closet to find something to wear for church. Like the lake, the church was a meeting ground for the entire town, and since Spirit Lake was a Christian community, every week most of the townspeople would gather together for worship. Every third Sunday during the warm months, everyone gathered in the park for the town's monthly community fellowship picnic. There would be an abundance of food on offer, a variety of sweets to delight in, and games for children and grown folks alike to enjoy. It was a Spirit Lake tradition and had been since the town was established in the 1800s.

Teylor looked forward to it every month, and today was no different. With all that had unfolded over the past week, she was excited to have some fun. She decided on a navy maxi dress and a camel-colored fedora. Her thick curls were tied in a low side ponytail to complement the hat. To finish the look, she slid on a pair of sandals the same shade as the fedora, hoop earrings, and a matte red lipstick to add a little color to the neutral palette on her face.

While Teylor sat down for a bowl of oatmeal before leaving, the conversation she and Rima previously had played in her mind. The thought of revealing her true feelings to Jamie was terrifying but deep down inside, she knew that Rima was right. Still how could she just come out and tell him—and what would be his response? He was engaged to another woman, and she was sure that he'd only ever looked at her as a little sister. She was even mad at herself for falling in love with him. If only she could look at him as a big brother, everything would carry on as normal, but she'd never looked at him that way and knew that she never would.

From the time they'd met in junior high, Teylor had known she'd never encounter another guy like him, and she hadn't. Jamie was Mr. Popular in school. Straight-A student, unbelievable athlete, and a favorite among hormonal teenaged girls. Teylor, on the other hand, remembered herself as a loner. Not that she couldn't make friends, rather she didn't because of her mom. Keeping the house in order kept her too busy for much socializing, and the embarrassment she would endure if someone came over and her mother was inebriated was too much of a risk, so she kept to herself.

Calvin, the school's tyrant, more often than not had something to say about her and her mother anyway though. Spirit Lake was a small town, and as much as her mom tried to conceal her addiction, people still talked. While Jamie's parents were respected throughout the town, what was said of her mother usually included the words "drunk" or "loose."

Teylor vividly recalled the day she and Jamie had officially met. She'd been in the line grabbing her lunch when Calvin approached her.

"Hey, Teylor, tell your mom she owes me a drink and a lap dance."

She heard the snickers of nearby students and was mortified. Tears welled up in her eyes, but Teylor wasn't going to let them see her cry. She had a hundred things she wanted to say to him but couldn't. It was already a task to maintain her composure and not break down in front of the entire cafeteria. She gathered herself and threw out the best comeback that came to mind.

"Screw you, Calvin."

"Whoa, big words for a small girl," he responded.

Calvin towered over her by at least four inches and outweighed her by eighty pounds. He lowered his face to hers and whispered, "But I think your mother has that covered. The screwing part, that is. You want to follow in her footsteps? I can be your first," he finished with a satisfied smile.

Teylor had had enough. She dropped her food tray on the floor and with all the strength she had, she drew back her open palm and connected with his face as hard as she could, forcing his head to jerk sideways from the impact.

The smack that echoed throughout the room was loud enough to silence the cafeteria. Calvin rubbed his face; his eyes were wide with shock. If that wasn't enough to piss him off, the "ooohs" and "ahhhs" from the crowd drove him over the edge. He drew his fist back to pound her while Teylor cringed in anticipation of the blow. But it never came.

When she opened her eyes, Calvin was lying on the floor and Jamie was standing over him, hands in fists. Calvin, apparently deciding he didn't want any more trouble, shot up and scurried away. Teylor, surprised that this popular guy who'd never spoken a word to her had come to her defense, managed to sputter out a muted "thank you" before hurrying outside to avoid further shame. She sat at a picnic bench alone and allowed a few tears to fall.

She was thankful for Jamie's help, but she felt humiliated—not to mention hungry after throwing her food on the floor—yet there was no way she was going to go back in there to face those people. She'd given them enough entertainment for one day. She'd rather starve.

Teylor wasn't sitting there long before a tray with a turkey sandwich, bag of chips, and iced tea was placed in front of her. She looked up and saw Jamie smiling. That was the first time she'd noticed his dimpled cheeks.

"Thought you might be hungry," he said.

She hesitated before saying, "You didn't have to do that. I'm not a charity case, you know."

He sat down across from her.

"I didn't say that you were. I just thought you might be hungry after throwing your food on the ground and slapping Calvin into next week," he said with a straight face.

She didn't want to but she laughed.

"That's nice."

"What?" she asked.

"Your smile. You're never smiling when I see you around. You should do it more often."

Their eyes held for a moment, and Teylor had to look away before her cheeks turned a brighter shade of red than they already were.

"Well, if I slapped him into next week, you definitely knocked him ahead a couple of generations."

They both laughed.

"Well," he replied, "consider this food a thank-you for giving me a reason to knock that punk out."

She nodded in agreement, split the sandwich, and gave him half.

"Well, if that's the case, consider this my payment for doing the job well."

That had been the beginning of their friendship and the moment she'd fallen in love with him.

After cleaning and putting away her dish, Teylor made up her mind. She was going to tell him. The loving and protective Jamie she knew would understand. Even if he didn't feel the same way, he'd be gentle with her heart. He always was.

~

It was a beautiful day for the church fellowship picnic. The weather was warm and the sun sat high in a cloudless sky. Pastor Nelson preached a wonderful sermon about loving one another, which was fitting seeing how she planned on revealing her true feelings to Jamie. Except she hadn't seen him during service. He never missed church unless there was an emergency, so she was sure that was the case, and if Jamie was in any kind of trouble, she needed to make sure things were okay. She set out to find him.

The park was buzzing with energy. Many of the games and tables had been assembled the day before. Folks gathered in laughter and excitement as the festivities started. Teylor spotted Ms. Lucy overseeing the food, making sure that everything was up to par.

Ms. Lucy, in her mid-sixties and a dead ringer for Margaret Avery, was wearing khaki knickerbockers with a white sleeveless button-down blouse. Her salt-and-pepper hair hung just below her ears in a stylish bob. She reminded Teylor of women from the fifties, classy and beautiful. Regal, but humble. Her diner had by far the best food Teylor had ever tasted in Arizona, and she was willing to bet Lucy'd give quite a few other places across the country a run for their money.

Mouthwatering dishes were spread out over six tables, and there were an extra two just for the desserts. Five wheel barrels loaded with ice and beverages were parked adjacent to the food. Teylor spotted Rima heading over to assist Ms. Lucy and went over to ask if she'd seen Jamie. Rima was removing tin foil from large trays of food when Teylor approached her.

Her fire-red locks were tied up into a high bun, and large bamboo earrings hung from her lobes. Her daisy-colored floor length wrap skirt and white off-the-shoulder top gave her the appearance of a bohemian goddess.

"Hey, Rima."

"Hey, girl," she said jovially. "Doesn't this food look amazing? I can't wait to get my hands on it."

"I bet you can't," Teylor said, laughing. Eating was one of Rima's favorite pastimes. She playfully rolled her eyes at Teylor.

"Hey, have you seen Jamie?"

Rima ate a grape from the fruit tray she'd just uncovered. "No, but I think I heard Charleston mention he went to the airport."

"Oh, his parents must be back in town." Rima shrugged and devoured a small cube of pineapple.

"Are you going to leave any of that for the others?" Teylor asked jokingly.

Rima, who'd already moved on to the perfectly cut watermelon slices, looked at Teylor and said, "Ha, ha. When do you go on tour with that stand-up? Since you're writing jokes and all."

Teylor shook her head at her friend. "I'll leave you to your fruit picking," she said, giggling. "I'm gonna go see if I can find Charleston."

Teylor scoured the park for Jamie's sister. She spotted her on a bench talking on her cell phone. As Teylor headed in her direction, Charleston saw her coming, ended the call, and hurried toward her.

"Hey, Charleston, have you—"

"Teylor, Jamie said he's been trying to reach you."

Teylor searched her purse for her cell but couldn't locate it.

"I must have left my phone at home. Is everything okay?" she asked nervously.

Charleston paused.

Teylor's pulse quickened. "Charleston, please, say something. Jamie's okay, isn't he?"

"Jamie's fine," she assured her.

Teylor sighed with relief. "So, what is it?"

"Jamie went to the airport."

"Yeah, Rima said you'd mentioned that. Are your parents back?"

Charleston shook her head.

"Charlie, just spit it out," Teylor demanded with a nervous chuckle. "Who's he picking up if not your parents?"

Before Charleston could answer, her attention was suddenly focused on something behind Teylor. Charleston met her eyes again and slowly turned her so that she could see for herself. Teylor went still. Jamie was walking hand in hand with an ebony beauty. Tall, slim, long jet black hair, with a smile as bright as the day's sun. Carrie.

She wore a crisp white jumpsuit that intimately hugged her slender body giving her the appearance of a runway model.

"He tried to tell you," Charleston whispered in her ear.

Teylor wanted to vomit. She'd prepared herself to tell Jamie that she was in love with him, and now here he was with the woman he loved. She wanted to make a run for it before he spotted her, but it was too late. They were quickly approaching. Charleston stood next to Teylor and planted a smile on her face.

"Relax, Teylor...and smile."

Before Teylor could gather her thoughts, Jamie and Carrie were standing before her. He leaned in and kissed Charleston on the cheek. "Hey, Charlie."

"Hey, little brother," Charleston responded with a nervous smile.

Jamie turned to Teylor and embraced her in a warm hug. He looked her in the eye ensuring that she was okay. She wasn't, but she wasn't about to show it. Not while the chocolate goddess was standing by his side. So Teylor forced a smile, letting him know that her emotions were under control, but it was of no use. He knew her too well, even better than she thought, and reluctantly he introduced his future bride to his sister and his best friend.

"Charlie, Teylor…this is Carrie."

Carrie wrapped her arms around Charleston, hugging her tightly. "I've heard so much about you," she gushed. Her speech was proper and had a mild New York City accent. "You're even more beautiful than your pictures."

"Thank you," Charleston said, smiling. "You're every bit as beautiful as Jamie said you were. It's nice to finally meet you."

Carrie flashed a genuine smile and focused her attention on Teylor.

"And, Teylor," she started, "I couldn't get Jamie to stop talking about you," she said, laughing. "It's nice to have a face to complement the stories he's always telling me. He speaks very fondly of you."

With a sheepish grin, Teylor offered her congratulations on their recent engagement and gave Jamie's fiancée a sincere embrace. Her heart was still breaking at the sight of them together but Carrie and Jamie weren't intentionally causing her pain, so until she could tell Jamie how she really felt, she would try her best to at least pretend to be happy for them.

Teylor felt Jamie's eyes on her, and she knew he was assessing the situation to make sure she was holding up okay. She couldn't understand how he could know she was falling apart on the inside, but not know why.

"So," Carrie said, clasping her manicured hands together. "I'm famished. Jamie dear, can we get something to eat?"

"Sure, sweetheart. Why don't we all go grab a plate and sit together," he responded, looking back and forth between the three women.

Charleston must have seen the pain in Teylor's eyes that she was so desperately trying to hide because she sought to rescue her. "Well, why don't you two go ahead? I'm sure you love birds have a lot of catching up to do."

"Are you kidding me? We just spent two weeks of uninterrupted quality time in Paris. We're good for now," Carrie insisted.

"Besides," she said, taking Jamie's hand in hers and meeting his gaze, "we have the rest of our lives to spend together."

Teylor swallowed the lump in her throat and half smiled. She was doing her best under the circumstances.

"Come with us," Carrie continued. "I want to get better acquainted with my new sisters."

The four of them piled their plates with barbequed chicken, potato salad, baked beans, corn on the cob, and fresh fruit. Then they sat at a long picnic table under a shade tree and dug in, all except Teylor and Jamie. She was about to take a bite of potato salad when she stopped herself. She whispered a thanksgiving prayer and then glanced at Jamie, who was already watching her. A slight smile played on his lips, and then he silently said his own prayer.

As they were eating and engaging in conversation, Ms. Lucy and Sandy walked over with ice-cold drinks and giddy smiles, excited about the sea of pleased faces grubbing hungrily on the food they'd prepared.

"How's everything, y'all?" Ms. Lucy asked as she sat the drinks on the table.

Living in Arizona for over thirty years hadn't managed to drown out her thick Southern accent, an audible reminder that she hailed from Houston. Every time it was mentioned, she'd reply, "You can take the girl outta the South, and you know the rest," with a charming smile—but that was Ms. Lucy, full of charm and Southern hospitality.

Everyone conveyed their approval of the food and gave thanks for the drinks.

"The temperature's climbing so y'all might wanna stay hydrated," she advised, placing her hands on her hips.

"This cuisine is very palatable, Ms. Lucy."

At the sound of Carrie's voice, Ms. Lucy and Sandy eyed her as if she were a strange bug they'd just noticed sitting at the table.

"Uh…Ms. Lucy, Sandy, this is Carrie…my fiancée," Jamie explained awkwardly.

Both Ms. Lucy's and Sandy's eyes bugged.

"Fiancée!" they shouted in unison.

Sandy quickly looked in Teylor's direction and back at Carrie. Teylor shifted in her seat and diverted her eyes elsewhere. Jamie looked embarrassed, while Carrie quickly extended her hand with a huge grin on her face.

"Nice to meet you both," she said.

Ms. Lucy eyed her hand for a nanosecond and then reluctantly shook it. Sandy followed suit.

"Where you from? Using words like 'cuisine' and 'palatable,' I know you ain't from nowhere 'round here."

"You are very astute. I was born in France to American parents, left there just shy of puberty, and flourished in Manhattan," Carrie replied. Her smile said she was humble but proud of her upbringing. Nothing wrong with that, Teylor thought.

"Flourished?" asked Sandy. "You mean you were raised in New York City?"

"Correct," Carrie replied.

Ms. Lucy nodded her understanding and directed her attention at Jamie. "Well, I guess congratulations are in order. Jamie, we can talk later because you know I have a hundred questions and I expect you to answer them all."

She was grinning but her eyes held a seriousness that assured Jamie she meant business.

Ms. Lucy was like a second mother to all of the town's residents under forty, and they knew not to test her. When she said "jump," they asked how high, but they always welcomed her godly and nurturing wisdom.

"I have to get back to my food and make sure nobody's fussing all over it. Y'all know how I hate people messin' in the food." She directed her attention back to Carrie. "It was nice to meet you, sweetheart." She then focused her eyes on Teylor, but spoke to the entire group.

"If you need anything else, anything at all, you know where to find me. Enjoy!"

She and Sandy headed back toward the food tables arm in arm. Teylor glanced over to see them both looking in her direction as they talked. She quickly glanced away, her gaze landing on Jamie's. He was studying her. Again. He'd been doing a lot of that lately. So protective of her heart, yet so far from knowing that he was the reason her heart needed protecting. She broke their gaze and went back to her food.

For a while, they all ate in silence, no one having anything to say after the awkward encounter with Ms. Lucy and Sandy. Finally, Carrie spoke.

"So, Teylor, Jamie tells me you're a writer."

Teylor nodded, mouth full.

"That's fascinating. I've always pondered the creative mind. I mean, being able to develop each character and make them relatable to a targeted audience. It's admirable. It'd be a very monotonous world without the arts."

After chewing and swallowing another forkful of potato salad, Teylor said, "Thank you, Carrie. I find a lot of joy in writing. It...um...gives me purpose, I guess." She shrugged.

"Wow, it's awe-inspiring that you live out your passion. I bet that makes you very good at it, doesn't it?"

Teylor laughed nervously. "I don't know about that."

"The modest Mahogany. She's better than good. She's an excellent writer," Jamie said, wiping his mouth with a napkin.

All three women froze and looked at Jamie. His eyes jumped back and forth between the three women, oblivious to the can of worms he'd just ripped open. Slightly amused, Charleston chuckled and took a sip of her iced tea.

Carrie eyed Teylor and then Jamie. "Mahogany?"

The faintest hint of realization graced Jamie's face when he became aware of what the estrogen in the group already knew. Teylor could see the wheels turning in his head as he desperately tried to find a way to dig himself out of the hole that his beloved nickname for her had just landed him in. Charleston must have also noticed the spinning wheels because she quickly came to the rescue.

"Mahogany is just a nickname we all call Teylor because of the color of her hair, eyes, and skin tone."

Carried nodded slowly and assessed Teylor. It was a good try but Teylor could tell that the other woman wasn't totally convinced. Regardless, Teylor was relieved when Carrie didn't question further and went back to nibbling on her food.

Over the next several minutes, the silence became deafening. Teylor grew tired of the awkwardness and was about to pretend she had to use the restroom when Rima approached their table with a sparkling smile and saved the day.

"Hey, guys."

To Teylor's surprise, Charleston was just as excited about the distraction as she was. Her voice raised a pitch higher than usual, she said, "Rima! Girl, have a seat. Please. We have someone we want you to meet."

SIX

Teylor was thankful for Rima's interjection and even more so for her interrogation of Carrie. There were so many unanswered questions circulating through her own head, and Rima was bent on getting answers to those same things. In the few minutes she'd been sitting, they'd learned that Carrie had attended an expensive private school, where she'd been cheerleader captain, a track star, captain of the debate team, valedictorian, prom queen, and modeled and appeared in several commercials.

Her parents were real estate moguls, which prompted her interest in the field, and she had joined their firm after getting her MBA. She spoke four languages, owned an apartment in Manhattan, a condo in Cabo, and was considering buying a flat in Paris after the wedding. She was the perfect wife on paper, but Teylor wondered if she was the perfect wife for Jamie. Carrie had a royal air about her. She was a high-profile businesswoman, a jetsetter, very confident in who she was and what she wanted—and she wanted Jamie.

The thought plagued Teylor, because she couldn't understand what a woman like Carrie, who exuded Paris, power connections, and wealth, wanted in Jamie, or more to the point, what he wanted with her. In Teylor's eyes, Jamie deserved the best of everything his heart could contain…and more. He loved the lake, old eighties and early nineties movies, soul food, and the Lord—which come to think of it, Teylor hadn't heard Carrie mention once.

"Are you saved, Carrie?" Teylor asked abruptly, interrupting the conversation between her and Rima.

All eyes fell on Teylor. She wasn't sure if they were surprised by the sudden outburst or the fact that she'd asked a very personal question. Jamie's mouth fell open, and he called Teylor's name like a parent scolding their child. Teylor's eyes darted to Jamie and back to Carrie.

"I'm sorry," she stated. "I didn't mean to be presumptuous. It's just that we're at the church picnic, and I was just curious."

Teylor cleared her throat and took a swig of her iced tea.

"You don't have to answer that," Jamie told Carrie. "Teylor didn't mean any harm. She's just nosy," he finished with a chuckle.

"And protective of you," Carrie whispered back.

Jamie quickly explained that coming to the picnic had been a last minute decision when Carrie had spotted the commotion on their way to her hotel.

More awkward silence ensued, and Jamie's and Teylor's eyes met again. Hers said that she was sorry for meddling and his said that it was okay.

"No, it's fine," Carrie spoke up. "I don't mind the question. I know you all want what's best for Jamie so I don't mind the interrogation," she quipped.

She fiddled with her napkin, which gave everyone the impression that Teylor had touched on an uncomfortable subject. Jamie gently clasped Carrie's hand, and it took everything within Teylor not to swat it like a fly on uncovered food.

"My parents are devout Catholics so of course, I followed suit. Go against the grain, you end up with splinters."

She fidgeted.

Jamie rubbed her back.

"Anyhow, we traveled to Vatican City annually for Easter. Christmas was biennial. My parents still go; that should tell you how important their religion is to them." She sipped her drink and continued.

"Me being the obedient child, I never interrogated them—my questions were numerous, but I just kept them bottled up. I didn't want to disappoint them, you know?" She smiled at Jamie and lovingly squeezed his hand. "Then I met Jamie and everything was…different."

"What do you mean?" Rima asked.

Carrie shrugged. "I mean that his relationship with God is unlike any I've ever encountered. It's genuine, unrehearsed…authentic. It's not the average day-to-day formula. He lives for it, every moment. It pours from his heart and I knew right away…I knew that whatever he and the Lord shared, I wanted for myself."

Jamie pulled Carrie close and kissed her forehead. She closed her eyes and reveled in his affection. Teylor was taken aback. She wanted to not like Carrie—nothing personal, she just wanted Jamie to herself—but here Carrie was winning them all over with her perfect performance. Jamie's face said she'd already won him. It was a sure thing. That hurt Teylor to the core, but maybe the time was drawing near. Maybe it was time to let Jamie go.

~

As the day carried on and the event wound down, some people started heading home. Many stayed behind to help clean the grounds. The women helped Ms. Lucy and Sandy pack up leftover food while the men gathered the tables and chairs to carry back to the church's basement. Children ran around collecting trash while Pastor Nelson promised candy to the ones who picked up the most, and Jamie took Carrie to the Spirit Lake Inn to find her a room.

When most of the work was done, Teylor retreated to a park bench to sit down. She was tired, more emotionally exhausted than anything, but she'd hope that those passing by would think she was tired from the events of the day and not sulking, which was what she was really doing. Rima, of course, was too smart for that. She headed Teylor's way, bamboo earrings swinging.

She sat on the bench next to Teylor and said nothing for a moment. They both just sat in silence and watched the remnants of another successful Spirit Lake picnic. Finally Rima peered at Teylor and said, "Not what you were expecting, huh?"

Teylor sighed. That was putting it mildly. "Clair Huxtable on steroids," she responded.

Rima giggled.

Teylor took her hat off, placed it in her lap, pulled out her low side ponytail, and ran her fingers through her curls.

"She's everything I'm not, Rima."

More silence filled the air. Rima leaned back and rested her elbows on the top of the bench. "She's definitely Paris," she said staring ahead at nothing in particular.

The same thing Teylor had thought earlier.

"And I'm…?" Teylor asked.

Rima paused.

"You? You're home. And trust me, T, there's no place like it."

~

Later that evening, Teylor showered and made a cup of hot vanilla chai. She cozied up on the couch and pressed play on the DVD remote. While the opening credits were rolling, her phone chirped, alerting her that she had a text message from Jamie.

Jamie: *U up?*

Teylor: *Yeah*

Jamie: *What are you doing?*

Teylor: *Goonies*

Jamie: *Be over soon.*

Teylor: *K*

Teylor paused the movie and waited, sipping and thinking. The fact that he was coming over to watch one of his favorite movies shouldn't be a surprise. He always did that, but things were different now. How would Carrie feel? Did she even know—or worse, was she coming with him? Teylor doubted it. He would never bring

Carrie without telling her first. Then again, he hadn't mentioned Carrie coming to Spirit Lake either, which really hurt Teylor. Things were changing by the minute, and once the "I do's" were spoken, what would become of her and Jamie then?

Twenty minutes later she heard a faint tapping at the front door. Force of habit. When they were younger, she'd sneak Jamie into her bedroom, and they'd stay up all night watching movies and talking. The light tapping at her bedroom window had been the signal that he'd arrived, and like then, her heart still raced with excitement every time she heard it. Some things never changed, but she knew change was coming soon. She could feel it.

She let him in, and they sat without saying a word. Her on the teal sofa, him on the adjacent cream recliner. She tossed him an olive throw and again pressed play on the movie. They watched without speaking, laughing here and there at the same parts they always laughed at. They'd seen the movie a hundred times and half of those times, they'd been together. Usually, they'd recite along with their favorite parts as if they knew all of the words by heart, but there was none of that tonight. There was an unspoken rhythm in the air that told truths of relationships being transformed. Hers and his being at the forefront. It scared the hell out of her, and she wondered if their hearts were still in sync. Was he just as frightened as she was?

Halfway through the movie, he spoke for the first time. "I'm sorry, Teylor. Had I known she was coming, I would've told you."

"You didn't know she was coming?"

"Not until she arrived."

Teylor thought it strange for Carrie to visit without letting him know that she was coming, but she decided to keep her thoughts to herself.

"So what do you think, TJ?"

She knew what Jamie meant but decided to ask anyway. "About what?"

"Carrie."

Teylor kept her eyes on the screen. "She's nice."

He sat up in the recliner and looked at her, but her eyes remained on the movie. "Anything else?"

Finally, she focused on him. "Like what?"

"She's nice? Kinda basic, don't you think? Give me details. I could see your wheels turning at the picnic earlier. What were you thinking?"

Teylor debated whether or not to tell him what she really thought. She and Rima had been thinking the same thing about Carrie being symbolic of Paris, but she didn't want Jamie to take it the wrong way. She didn't want him to think that she was jealous— even though she was, she wasn't ready to reveal it just yet. In the end, she settled on the truth. They'd always been honest with one another, except when it came to the little fact of how she truly felt about him.

"Honestly?" she asked.

He nodded. "Honestly."

"She's Paris."

He frowned in confusion. "Meaning?"

"You know how Paris is. It's Paris," she stated, throwing her hands up in a grand gesture. "That's what she reminds me of."

Jamie chuckled and shook his head. "Teylor, you've never been to Paris. How would you know?"

"You don't have to have been there to know what it's like. Everyone talks enough about it to where you just know," she responded defensively.

"Okay, humor me. Describe Carrie, or should I say Paris, in so many words."

Teylor sat up and took a deep breath.

"Okay," she said. "Beautiful, elegant, fashionable, brilliant, charming, exotic, sophisticated, romantic. Need I go on?"

"No, I get your point."

He smiled and shook his head slowly. She could sense what was coming next and that he was debating if he should ask or not. He decided on the former.

"So what am I?"

The same question Teylor had asked Rima about herself. She perched her elbow on the sofa's back and rested the side of her face in her palm. He waited, refusing to break eye contact.

"You're...Spirit Lake," she said finally.

Jamie cocked his head to the side and squinted. "Spirit Lake?"

"Yeah, Spirit Lake."

"Okay, I'll entertain your opinion for a moment instead of jumping to conclusions."

"Why would you jump to conclusions? You're acting like I insulted you."

"No. I didn't say that. But what are you saying? That I'm not good enough for Paris?"

Teylor's mouth fell open. "What? No! I would never say that—or even think it!" She lowered her voice. "Jamie, you deserve everything that God has for you. Everything. Whatever that may be. Paris is all of those things that I mentioned but Spirit Lake is...Spirit Lake is loving, protective, safe, enchanting, mesmerizing, blessed, and filled with the spirit of God. All those things that Carrie said about your relationship with God—she was right. You make everyone around you want to know Him. Paris is a beautiful place to experience, I'm sure, but Spirit Lake is home."

He was silent, but he kept his eyes on her. Her cheeks flushed and she looked away.

Jamie smirked and stood. "I should be going, Teylor."

She rose from the couch to face him. "What? Why? Are you upset?"

"It's just late, Teylor, and I'm tired. Gotta lot going on this week, and I need to rest up."

"Are you sure? You can sleep in the spare room, like you normally do."

He gave her a soft peck on the cheek. "I'll see you later," he said and walked out the front door.

Teylor stood there and watched the door until she heard his car leave. A dreaded feeling came over her. One that she knew was coming but had still hoped wouldn't. Now, hope was fading. It was happening. Change had begun.

SEVEN

"*Jamie, I need a break.*"

Teylor was bent over with her gloved hands on her knees, breathing rapidly. Fog exited with every exhale, a sure sign, in her opinion, that it was too cold to be outside hiking.

"*You're such a rookie. How many times have we done this and you still haven't built up enough endurance to get to the top of this mountain?*"

Jamie chuckled at his own banter.

They were midway to the top of Spirit Mountain, and Teylor had had about all she could take. She rolled her eyes at Jamie, too tired to crack back. She was using all of her energy to catch her breath. Jamie shook his head in amusement.

"*Here,*" he said, handing her a bottle of water. "*Am I going to have to carry you the rest of the way?*" He was having too much fun with this.

She managed to choke out a mangled "hush" before standing straight and taking a sip of water.

"*You know, I'm going to have to replace you if you keep holding me back like this. I'm trying to get a decent workout in,*" he quipped.

Teylor squirted water at him from the bottle. He dodged the liquid and erupted in laughter.

"*Hey, it's too cold out here for all of that,*" he shouted.

"Well, you're the smart guy who wanted to hike in the middle of November."

Mirth was dancing in his eyes. Watching her struggle up the paved hill gave him pure delight.

"Well, it's almost Thanksgiving, and you know how you eat during the holidays. I'm just doing you a favor."

Teylor charged at him, and he took off running. He ran in circles, laughing as she playfully swung at him, missing every time. She wore herself out even more and had to sit down on the pavement to catch her breath. Jamie thought he would die from laughing so hard.

"That's it," she said between breaths. "I'm done. I'm going back down and going home."

Jamie held up the car keys with a huge grin on his dimpled face. "Are you planning to walk home or hitchhike?"

Teylor frowned. "I hate you so much."

"Hate's a strong word, T."

"Maybe, but it's so fitting right now."

He chuckled and sat down beside her. He wrapped an arm around her shoulders and kissed her on the cheek.

"Nope. It's too late to try and be Mr. Nice Guy now," she said, pulling away.

Jamie was having too much fun teasing her. It was nothing new. Every time they hiked, Teylor would take too many breaks, and he would poke fun at her the entire time. But she always tried again. The beautiful tall pine trees covered the mountain like a canopy. Their enormity blocked the sun, but refusing to be outdone, the biggest star in the sky cast its beams through the branches, hitting the forest's dirt floor. The splendor of it left Jamie awestruck. Hiking was something he loved—Teylor, not so much, but she came anyway...for him.

"I'll make you a deal, Mahogany. If you make it to the top, I'll not only buy you a steaming cup of vanilla chai, but I'll also throw in a slice of carrot cake, and get this...I won't ask you to come back here all winter."

"I accept, but I want whipped cream and caramel on that chai."

"Deal." Jamie chuckled and stood. He held out his hand to help her up. "Come on, sweets. Let's knock this out."

~

Jamie admired the pines as he made his way uptown. He hadn't been hiking since that day last November with Teylor. He missed it and reminded himself that he'd have to go back soon, but he wasn't sure it would be with her. He still wasn't clear about where their relationship was headed and that bothered him. He needed help sorting things out, and he was heading for the one person who could help him make sense of things.

When Jamie pulled up to his parents' house, his mother was outside watering her rosebushes. As soon as she saw him, a huge grin spread across her yellow-brown face showcasing the deep dimples that she'd passed along to him. Gail Westbrook was a timeless beauty. Her hair had grayed prematurely, and Jamie couldn't remember it being any other shade than the stunning silver it was now. Gail had given up relaxers while Jamie was still in high school, and the tight silver coils that hung to her jawline had become her signature look. In her mid-fifties and in great shape, she looked ten years younger, but radiated the wisdom of ancient queens.

Jamie hopped out of the car, ran up the paved walkway, and wrapped his mother in a tight hug, lifting her off the ground. When her feet touched earth again she snuggled his face in her palms.

"How's my baby boy doing?"

His eyes dropped, and he gave a half smile. Mrs. Westbrook leaned away from him, her dark almond eyes piercing his.

"That bad, huh?"

"Could be worse." Jamie knew what was coming next and he welcomed it.

Gail grabbed her only son by the hand and led him in the house. He needed to talk and she was ready to listen.

They sat at the table in the breakfast nook, the same one that he and Charleston had sat at just over a week earlier. This time, there was no staring at the ceiling. He focused on his mother's loving eyes. Concerned and knowing, she had a way of penetrating his thoughts and understanding exactly what he was feeling before he said a word. He took a sip of the ice cold lemonade she set before him. The day was warm, and the cool liquid was refreshing. He inhaled...exhaled, threw a smile her way. She stuck a finger in his dimple and he laughed. She'd been doing that since he was a small boy. It still had the same effect on him.

"How was your and Dad's trip, gorgeous?"

"Wonderful, as always. Your aunt Charlie 'bout drove me crazy, but we made it without harming one another, praise the Lord." She threw a hand in the air in praise.

Jamie laughed and said, "And I bet you miss her already."

"Of course!"

They both erupted in laughter. Gail's smile faded, and she placed her hand on Jamie's knee.

"So, sweetheart, could this solemn mood have anything to do with your recent engagement?"

Jamie gave her a "how did you know?" look, but she shook her head, unwilling to reveal her sources. Jamie half rolled his eyes.

"Charlie and her rampant mouth."

"Nope. Believe it or not, when it comes to you, your sister can keep a secret."

"Then who?"

"That's not important, Jamie."

His face relaxed in realization. "Ms. Lucy," he said knowingly. "Sometimes I forget you are two peas in a pod."

She remained quiet, letting Jamie know he'd assumed correctly.

"Sorry I didn't tell you, Mom. I wanted to wait until you and Dad came back. Didn't want to lay the news on you while you were away from home."

"It's okay, son. I know you meant well. You always do."

She studied him for a moment. Knowing her son had a protective nature, she understood how hard it was for him to share his burdens with his loved ones. Usually, he'd find a way to deal with it, not wanting to cause worry to the people he cherished most, and even though he was reluctant now, Gail could clearly see the pain he was feeling. Being his mother, she'd seen him at his best and his worst, but the look on his face now she'd seen many times before. It was synonymous with one person: Teylor.

"So…why so glum for such a happy occasion? Or is it not as happy as you thought it would be?"

"The latter."

"I see. Could the reason it's not such a happy occasion have anything to do with Teylor?"

Jamie threw his hands up and let them fall back to his lap. "How does everyone know that?" he asked, frustrated.

"How could you not, son?"

Jamie placed his elbow on the table and massaged his temples with his thumb and middle finger.

Gail pulled his hand away from his face and raised his chin to meet her eyes. "Sweetheart, did you really think she'd take it well?"

He shrugged. "I—"

"And before you answer that, keep in mind that I know you better than anyone else, besides the good Lord. So be honest with yourself because I already know the answer."

Jamie's gaze fell to the floor. "It was all I could think about when I was proposing. How she'd react. If she'd be hurt. That's the last thing I'd ever want to do to her, but it's the only thing I've been able to accomplish lately."

He took a deep breath and met his mother's worried gaze. "I can see it in her eyes, Mom, every time I look at her. Her pain is evident and it's all my fault."

Gail placed Jamie's hand in hers. "Don't blame yourself, honey. You've always been her champion, and you and I both know you would never intend to hurt her. As long as your intentions were pure, you have to forgive yourself for what you have no control over. You're in control of your decisions, but you have no control over the reactions of others to your decisions."

"So what now? How do I fix it?"

She gave him a curious look. "Let me ask you something, Jamie. You love Carrie, right?"

"Right."

"Then why is it that when you were proposing to her, the first person you thought about was Teylor?"

He thought a moment before answering. "I don't know. She's my best friend and I care about how she feels."

"Is that all?"

He remained silent.

"I'm confident, son, that those dimples aren't the only things God gave us alike. You are full of wisdom. I know you'll figure this out, and when you do, everything will fall in perfect order."

She kissed his cheek and rose from her seat.

Holding out her hand, she said, "Now come on. Let's go and see what your father is up to."

~

Teylor stared at the blinking cursor on the computer screen. Ideas ran through her mind like wildebeests during a stampede, but she couldn't force them into words. Distractions also had their part in her lack of productivity, but try as she might, she couldn't rid herself of them. She started on the back porch and then found her way to the kitchen. When neither of those worked, she ended up in a spare room that she used as a writing office. Inspiration flowed everywhere, but getting it down on paper was a task.

Teylor threw her face in her hands and massaged her eyes with her fingertips.

"Focus, Teylor. Focus, Teylor. Focus, Teylor," she chanted to herself.

What was she even supposed to be writing about? When she'd first decided that she was going to write a novel, she'd thought she had the perfect synopsis, but she was ashamed to admit that the furthest she'd gotten was writing two words: *chapter one.*

Who was she kidding? She wasn't getting anything done today either, not with Jamie and Carrie weighing heavily on her mind. Last night hadn't gone well, and she kept replaying the events over and over in her head. Why was Jamie so offended? Why didn't he stay? He always stayed. She was also annoyed that Carrie had decided to pop up out of the blue without so much as a warning or an invitation for that matter, and then had the audacity to crash the church's picnic. Did she ever consider that maybe Jamie wasn't ready to introduce her to the people in his life?

Teylor rolled her eyes and walked away from her laptop. She wasn't in the mood for writing. She was in the mood for cake.

~

When Teylor opened the glass door to Songbird Café, the aroma of caffeinated dreams hit her like a strong wind. Wearing navy sweats, a white T-shirt, and sneakers, with her hair swept up into her signature high bun, she entered the heavenly scented haven and found Rima standing behind the counter positioned to the left of the café. Cakes, pies, scones, cookies, and pastries were beautifully arranged in the glass case beneath the countertop. On the wall behind the counter were three large black chalkboards displaying the names and prices of a selection of caffeinated and decaffeinated beverages.

Rima, dressed in a turquoise romper and gold hoops, with her red locks pinned to one side, waved happily when she spotted her. Teylor took a seat in the café next to the window. While she waited for Rima to bring her usual order, hot vanilla chai and a slice of carrot cake, Teylor took in the array of colors in the café. A mixture of red, gold, green, yellow, blue, and black danced on the walls. Red chandeliers hung sporadically from the ceiling, and a decent number of black tables and chairs were placed strategically throughout on the polished pearl-tiled floor. The sounds of Sade's *By Your Side* whispered through the speakers, and Teylor swayed along to the music in her seat. Besides the bookstore, Rima's café was one of her favorite places to write when she came into town. It modeled her friend's personality to a tee. Beautiful, colorful, and soulful.

"No writing today?"

Rima placed the tea and cake in front of Teylor and sat down in the seat across from her.

"Wasn't feeling it today. Just wanted tea and cake."

"Well, either way, I'm glad to see you. How have you been?"

Teylor held the mug with both hands and blew the hot liquid before taking a sip.

"Good," she said placing the cup back on the table. She picked up a fork and went for the slice of cake. She knew Rima was getting ready to ask her about Jamie and Carrie, and she just didn't have the strength to deal with the conversation. She decided to focus on another topic. Any topic.

"Where's Connie?"

Connie was the baker at the café. Rima was a pro at making the beverages and hiring entertainment, but when it came to the baking, she was no Betty Crocker. Connie, a forty-something, self-taught culinary genius, was the magic behind the sweet treats. Born and raised on the Navajo reservation, she'd found her way to Spirit Lake by accident. Headed toward Phoenix on a cold winter's night, her truck was loaded with all of her belongings, and she was looking for new beginnings. When her tire blew on the I-17 about twenty miles south of Flagstaff, the excitement she'd harbored about starting a new life in a big city quickly dwindled.

She'd tell you now that the Lord must have been watching over her because Pastor Nelson, driving home from a men's conference in Albuquerque, saw her stranded on the side of the road one mile shy of his exit. A winter storm was beginning to set in, so instead of changing her tire, he offered to take her to the nearest hotel, which just so happened to be located in Spirit Lake, and come back for her car the next morning.

In December, Spirit Lake resembles a town straight out of a snow globe. Snow covers the ground, tall trees, and mountains. The buildings and streetlamps glitter all over from the Christmas décor that adorns the entire town. Carolers are caroling, children are sledding, and folks are filled with holiday cheer. For Connie, that first night in Spirit Lake was unlike anything she'd ever experienced, and she knew right away the Lord had brought her there for a purpose. That had been ten years ago. She never made it to Phoenix and to this day, holds no regrets.

"I gave her a couple of hours off to tend to some personal matters. She came in early to make the goodies you see in the case over there, so they're fresh," Rima said, pointing to the delicacies Teylor had spotted when she'd walked in.

"She'll be back before the lunch rush to make more."

"This cake is delicious. That girl knows she can do wonders with flour and sugar," Teylor said, taking another bite.

"That's why I hired her."

"I still don't know how you managed to get her in here," Teylor confessed, taking another bite. "Everybody in town tries to hire her to make everything from breakfast croissants to wedding cakes. I don't see how she finds the time to come here and work for you."

"All she does is bake. She loves it. It's a passion, kinda like you with writing, except she bakes more than you write," Rima joked.

Teylor laughed, picked a walnut from her cake, and tossed it at Rima. She was about to offer her friend a good explanation for her recent lack of writing when she noticed Rima's smile fading. Her expression became grim as she stared past Teylor, looking out the window. Teylor turned to see what had suddenly dimmed her mood and when she saw it, her face instantly matched Rima's.

There they were, Carrie and Jamie, hand in hand, walking across the street looking like the newlyweds they were yet to be. Seeing them together in that way reminded Teylor of the couple she'd seen walking into the bookstore when she was having lunch with Jamie at Lucy's. Knowing that it was them together and not her and Jamie felt like a dagger going through her heart. Her appetite quickly vanished.

Teylor faced Rima again and slowly pushed her cake away. She took small sips of her chai and tried to erase what she'd just witnessed. Why did she feel like crying all of a sudden, and when would she get past the hurt?

"Are you okay?" Rima asked her.

Tired of lying about how she really felt, Teylor shook her head. "I'm hoping I will be soon, but..." She shrugged.

"Are you still planning to tell him?"

Another shrug.

"What changed?"

65

Teylor laid out everything that had happened the night before, ending with how he'd left instead of staying the night like he usually did.

"Things are different now, Rima. It was bound to happen."

"Things are going to be different anyway."

"You've already said that," Teylor responded, referring to the last conversation they'd had on her back porch.

"I'm not talking about that."

"Then what *are* you talking about?"

"What do you want, Teylor? Do you want things to be the same between you and Jamie? BFFs forever? Or do you want a romantic relationship with him, because that will change things as well.

"One of two things is going to happen. One"—Rima held up her index finger—"he's going to marry Carrie and the BFF thing will be over for the two of you. Two," she continued, holding two fingers in the air, "you'll discover, after telling him how you really feel, that he feels the same way about you and you will live together in eternal bliss. Either way, the relationship you two have now is going to change, and you, my pretty curly-haired friend, are going to have to get used to it."

Teylor sat there speechless. What Rima said hurt, but she also knew it to be the truth. It was time for her to grow up. They weren't little Jamie and Teylor in junior high anymore. They'd both grown into mature adults with very adult feelings, and she had to face it, regardless of the outcome. Teylor had never thought she could handle losing her mother, but here she was, thriving by the grace of God. If He pulled her through that, He'd see her through anything.

Teylor inhaled deeply and said, "You're right. Again. I hate it, but you are."

Rima giggled, and Teylor found herself smiling again.

"I have to stop making excuses. Stop running from myself. I'll face it, Rima. I have to."

Rima glanced over Teylor's shoulder again.

"I'm glad you said that. You can right start now—they're coming this way."

EIGHT

R ima greeted Jamie and Carrie as they entered the café. Carrie looked stunning in a long emerald wrap dress and diamond studded sandals. Her coal-colored tresses hung loosely down her back. Teylor thought Jamie looked handsome in everything he wore. Today, he chose dark-blue jeans; a fitted gray T-shirt, which accentuated his toned physique; and matching gray suede loafers.

The three of them walked to the counter so that Jamie and Carrie could order. Rima pointed toward the restrooms, and Carrie took off in that direction. Neither Carrie nor Jamie had spotted Teylor when they'd entered. She saw Rima point her way, and when Jamie turned and saw her, a look of regret shadowed his face. Teylor flashed a half smile and looked away. It was time for her to leave, but before she could gather her satchel, Jamie walked over and occupied the seat Rima had vacated.

"Hey, T."

"Hey," she responded plainly without making eye contact. She fumbled through her purse, pretending to be looking for something.

"How are you?" he asked.

Teylor wasn't in the mood for fictitious small talk and she let him know it.

"I'm sorry to intrude. I didn't know you'd be here. God forbid I'd want a cup of tea," she snapped.

Jamie's face froze in bewilderment. "What are you talking about?"

"My eyes work, Jamie. I saw your face when you looked over and saw that I was here, and please don't insult my intelligence by trying to deny it. It'll only make things worse."

Jamie's eyes dropped to the floor, then he shot a quick glance in the direction of the restrooms. Teylor knew he was looking to see if Carrie was coming. This time when he looked at her, her sad eyes met his.

"You're right, but it's not what you think. It's not that I'm not happy to see you, I just don't want to see you hurt."

Teylor shook her head, not believing him.

"It's true, Teylor. Things have been different with you and me...For someone that I thought I knew better than myself, I'm having a hard time figuring you out. I don't know how to make things...to make us...like we used to be."

Teylor fought back tears. Things *were* different and for the life of her, she couldn't understand why he didn't realize that he was the reason why.

"Why are they different?" she asked.

"That's what I've been trying to figure out, but you won't give me a straight answer. You haven't been yourself lately."

Their eyes held in silence.

Finally Teylor spoke, her voice softer than she'd intended. "Maybe things can't be like they were."

"Why would you say something like that?"

Apprehensive about her next statement, she held her tongue. He waited.

"You left last night, Jamie."

"After you said Carrie was too good for me."

"I never said that."

"Not in so many words. Paris and Spirit Lake. Remember?"

"I don't see the offense. Is that so bad?"

"It is when you compare a luxurious city with a small town."

"You don't get it," she said, shaking her head and staring out the window.

"Well, explain it to me."

Teylor kept quiet. Jamie saw Carrie coming out of the restroom and smiled at her as she approached. Rima called her to the counter to pick up their orders. He kept his eyes on Carrie and said, "I'm wearing thin, Teylor. This game of tug-of-war we've got going on…it's wearing me out. I'm hanging on by a thread."

He focused his gaze back on Teylor. "Just say it. Whatever it is, I can handle it. We've gotten through tougher situations than this."

Teylor went still. Those three words she'd been wanting to say for years sat on the tip of her tongue. Yet fear took over and made her mute, and even more frightening, she could have sworn that he was waiting for it, as if he'd given her an invitation to reveal her passion for him. Refusing to break eye contact, his stare beckoned her, but once again Teylor ran away from the opportunity. She made a beeline for the door without so much as a goodbye to Rima or a hello to Carrie.

~

Teylor made it back across the lake in record time. Just as she was walking through her back door, she received a text from Rima.

Rima: *Girl, what was that about?*

Teylor: *Nothing. Tell you about it later.*

Rima: [Rolling eye emoji]

Teylor: *I know. Same old shenanigans.*

Rima: *Well, Jamie wanted me to tell you about the get-together at his place tonight. Said you left before he could.*

Teylor sat her phone down on the kitchen counter and went to lay down on the living room sofa. She couldn't respond to Rima's text about Jamie's gathering right now. Not after what'd just happened. He hadn't even mentioned it to her. Did he really want her there? Then again, why wouldn't he? Things were awkward between them, but she was still his best friend. They still shared a bond that neither of them had with anyone else. She thought about what he'd said earlier.

Just say it.

"Just say what?" she asked herself aloud.

She heard her phone chirping in the kitchen and decided she'd deal with it later. She closed her eyes to clear her mind and before she knew it, she'd drifted off to sleep.

Teylor awakened to bright sunlight streaming through the windows. She forced herself off the couch and walked into the kitchen to check the time. The clock on the wall said it was one o'clock in the afternoon. She'd slept over two hours. Her stomach started growling, and she realized she'd only had a slice of carrot cake and chai tea for breakfast earlier. After eating a turkey and avocado sandwich and gulping down a tall glass of water for lunch, Teylor set out to get some writing done on her back porch.

She managed to write and submit an article to the editor of a journal she freelanced for, outline and set a deadline for the next article that would be due, and complete a chapter of her novel before she decided to call it quits for the day. By the time she glanced at the clock again, it was almost five o'clock in the evening. She noticed her phone sitting on the counter where she'd left it before falling asleep and decided to check for messages from Rima. When she looked at the screen, she had five messages from Rima and two from Jamie. She opened Rima's first:

Rima: *Hello?*

Rima: *So you're just going to ignore my messages?*

Rima: *Hello?*

Rima: *Fine...* [Angry face emoji]

Rima: *His place. 7 pm. In case you decide to come.*

Jamie: *Hey. Rima said she told you.*

Jamie: *My place at 7. Please come.*

Teylor walked into the living room and stared at the DVD player. She could go to Jamie's and continue to perform the same song and dance routine, or she could snuggle up on her comfortable couch, pop some popcorn, and watch old movies. She opted for the latter.

After popping the popcorn on the stove, she decided on the first movie and inserted it into the DVD player. A bright green error message flashed across the player.

"You've got to be kidding me."

She ejected the DVD and re-inserted it, repeating the process three more times with increasing annoyance. The same error message danced in front of her after each attempt.

"Ugh!"

She plopped on the couch and sighed. "Lord, is this some kind of a joke?"

She sat idle for a few more minutes and re-weighed her options. That two-and-a-half-hour nap ensured that she'd be awake for hours and hours. Not wanting to spend the rest of the night buried behind her laptop, she headed toward the shower to get ready for Jamie's.

NINE

"Whom did you invite, darling?" Carrie asked as she uncovered the catered food Jamie had ordered from Lucy's.

"The regulars. Saber, Rima, Charlie and Jonathan, Teylor."

Jamie walked over to join Carrie and inspect the contents of the foil pans. "Man, this looks ridiculously good," he said, pleased with what he saw.

"It does, but do you guys always eat like this? It's so fattening."

"Not always, but an indulgence every once in a while doesn't hurt," he said and gave her a playful kiss on the nose.

Ms. Lucy had prepared fried chicken, collards, candied yams, sweet cornbread, fresh biscuits, and peach cobbler at Jamie's request. Jamie started prepping beverages for his soon-to-arrive guests as Carrie continued to examine the food.

"Why have two different types of bread, Jamie?"

Jamie shrugged. "Different folks, different strokes."

"I guess," she mumbled to herself. Louder she added, "I wasn't brought up eating soul food. My mother deemed it slave food."

"I'm sure if you had the opportunity to ask any slave, they'd have appreciated a meal like this. They were far more deprived, Carrie."

She smiled and he placed a light kiss on her lips. She wrapped her arms around his neck, wanting to linger in his personal space. He stared into her half-closed eyes and saw the heat of passion staring back at him.

"My desire to make love to you grows stronger every time you kiss me," she confessed.

Jamie took a step back. "Then I'm going to have to stop kissing you."

Carrie opened her eyes fully and let out a soft gasp.

"Don't look at me like that," he said. "You know the deal."

"I know," she said, pouting. "But we're going to be married anyway. What's the difference?"

"The difference is, we're not married *yet*, Carrie."

He caressed the side of her face, and her eyes momentarily closed.

"Come on, babe. Don't do this. You know how important it is to me that we wait."

He kissed her again, this time on her forehead. He didn't want to provoke any more temptation than he already had. Because he'd practiced abstinence for so long, he'd gained a respectable amount of self-control in that area of his life, but oftentimes he forgot that it proved to be a weakness for others. He decided to give her some space and went back to preparing the drinks for the gathering.

"I've never met anyone like you, Jamie. So much restraint."

He chuckled and turned to face her. "Trust me, it takes a lot of Jesus to keep me in line. I desire to make love to you every time I see you, Carrie, but I desire more to please my heavenly Father, and to protect you at all costs. If I have sex with you now, it will only tarnish what the Lord has in store for us. I want everything He has prepared for us, and in order to get it, I have to be obedient to His Word."

She grinned from ear to ear and walked toward him, lips puckered as if to give him a deep kiss on the lips. Before she could get near, he wagged his finger and said, "Nope. There's too much heat in this kitchen."

They both laughed and went back to preparing for the party. As Jamie was arranging the last of the drinks on the counter, his thoughts traveled to Teylor. He hoped she'd come, in spite of their previous conversation. He wasn't sure where they were headed, but he wasn't ready to let go of what they shared. Things were definitely changing between them, but he was still hopeful that he could mend the rip that was beginning to tear them apart.

"Jamie," Carrie said, snapping him out of his thoughts. He turned to see her staring at him like she'd just discovered the cure for cancer.

"Why wait, darling?"

Jamie shook his head in disbelief. "You are incorrigible, woman. I just explained—"

"No, not that," she said, interrupting him. "I meant, why wait to get married? Why not do it sooner?"

"What are you talking about? A year is already sooner. Carrie, we haven't even discussed where we'll live. What about your career, and mine? You live in New York, remember? I can't just pick up my business and move across the country. Are you willing to move here?"

Carrie sighed. "Jamie, darling, we don't have to have it all figured out right now. I have a little leeway to do what I please as far as my career is concerned."

"Yeah, I've noticed," Jamie mumbled under his breath.

"And what is that supposed to mean?" Carrie snapped.

Jamie shook his head. He wanted to tell her that he'd noticed that she packed up and went wherever she chose and whenever she chose to, with little regard for work or money, not to mention, he hadn't seen her so much as open a laptop or take a client's phone call since she'd been in Spirit Lake, but he thought better of it and kept his mouth shut. There was no need to spark an argument right before his friends were set to arrive.

"Darling," Carrie said in a calmer voice, "we will have forever to figure out our lives, but I'm ready to do it together. Let's get married sooner."

"How soon are we talking?" Jamie said through an exhaled breath.

She bit her bottom lip. "Next week?"

"Next week! Woman, have you lost your mind?"

"Jamie, why not? We're going to marry either way, right?"

"Well, yeah, but—"

"But what? Are you planning on changing your mind?"

"No, Carrie. It just seems rushed. We can't plan a wedding that soon. And what about your parents?"

"My parents can charter a plane in seconds. And we can have a small, intimate ceremony here in Spirit Lake, just your closest loved ones and my parents. Then we can figure out all the details of our lives together and have the grand wedding next year, like we planned."

Jamie thought about it. He wasn't sure it was the best idea. First, he'd have to consider his parents. They wouldn't take this sudden change well, and second…Teylor. She'd take it even worse. As much as he wanted to protect everyone's feelings, he realized that his own were suffering. He couldn't go on trying to make everyone else happy, while his own happiness sat idle. Carrie walked over to him and wrapped her arms around his waist.

"Please, Jamie? Aren't you ready to wake up next to each other every morning? To finish torturing ourselves with wanting each other? We could make love whenever we wanted." She smiled seductively. "And as often as we wanted. We could sleep in the same bed together, and have breakfast together every morning. Aren't you ready to start our lives together?"

He ran his fingers through her hair. "You can be so convincing, you know that?"

Another smile from her.

"Okay," he said. "Let's do it."

~

Teylor decided to drive over the bridge instead of taking the boat across the lake. She reached town in fifteen minutes and was pulling into the parking garage of Jamie's building five minutes after that. At seven forty-five the sun was setting and the temperature had dropped, which prompted Teylor to throw a jean jacket over her gray leggings and white loose tank. She'd also opted for camel-colored ankle boots instead of sandals. She wore her thick curls in the same signature high bun and large gold hoops dangled from her earlobes. She gave her face a once-over in the rearview mirror, making sure her magenta lipstick hadn't smeared, before stepping out of the car.

Nerves played in her stomach as she took the elevator to Jamie's luxurious condo. When she reached the top floor, she heard laughter and music coming from his apartment. Teylor paused in front of Jamie's door and took a deep breath. She'd purposely left the key to his apartment at home because she didn't feel comfortable letting herself in while Carrie was visiting. Another inhale, slow exhale, and then she knocked.

A beat later, the door swung open. Jamie, clad in straight-leg blue jeans and a short-sleeved button-down shirt with black cuffs, appeared delighted to see her.

"Teylor." A smile of relief took over his face. "I'm happy you came."

He pulled her in and embraced her. Despite their encounter earlier, he seemed genuinely pleased that she was here, and the feeling of being in his arms made her insides melt.

"Thanks for inviting me, Jamie," she said, smiling.

"Well, it wouldn't be a party without you. Why'd you knock? Where's your key?"

The look in Teylor's eyes explained everything.

He nodded, understanding. "Well, come on, everyone's been waiting for you."

Teylor stepped in to the chorus of Mint Condition's *Pretty Brown Eyes* flowing through the surround sound. She laughed to herself because she thought the lyrics suited her mood. Over the past few days, she'd contemplated throwing herself at Jamie's feet and begging him to quit breaking her heart, but where would that leave her other than looking desperate and pathetic. She'd keep her dignity for now.

Jamie's condo was a modern, moderately masculine, and stylish haven. Teylor had been there more times than she could count, and she never tired of the debonair décor. The view of the town that the floor to ceiling windows captured always left her mesmerized. She stole a glance at one of Jamie's most valued possessions, a polished black grand piano that had belonged to his paternal grandfather.

Teylor had sat in this room many times, attempting to sing along as Jamie played songs on the piano.

"Have you played lately?" she asked, pointing in the direction of the piano.

"No. Maybe tonight. We'll see."

She wondered where their relationship was heading. The moments she'd shared with Jamie had defined the joy in her life. The thought of losing what they shared weighed heavy on her heart, but Teylor was determined to get through the night without incident, so she gathered her composure and impersonated happiness.

When they entered the kitchen and den area, Teylor spotted their usual friends eating, laughing, and enjoying the music.

"Look who's here!" Jamie yelled.

Everyone shouted their hellos as Teylor entered. Carrie, looking stunning as usual in a black fitted floor length dress, sat on the sectional talking to Charleston, who looked casually cute in ripped jeans and a sky-blue silk top. Her husband, Jonathan, was nowhere to be found. Rima, of course, was in the kitchen loading her plate with more food. She was also casually dressed in skinny jeans and a red tank top that matched the candy-red tresses tumbling loosely down her back. Teylor walked over to her.

"I see you came," Rima said, biting into a piece of chicken.

"Might as well."

"Jamie was expecting you. He even got your favorite," she whispered, pointing toward Ms. Lucy's biscuits.

Teylor kept quiet, however, the fact that he'd ordered biscuits when he'd already had sweet cornbread said he'd anticipated her coming. She smiled inwardly but didn't dare give Rima the satisfaction of teasing her.

"Go on," Rima urged. "Grab a plate."

Teylor took a little of everything, except dessert and cornbread, and sat on a stool next to Rima. She looked around the room. Jamie poked his head out onto the terrace and yelled at Saber to come back in.

"Saber's here?" she asked Rima.

Rima rolled her eyes. "Unfortunately."

Saber came in from the terrace, his green eyes piercing hers. A huge grin spread across his face, making him look boyish despite his sophisticated attire of black slacks, white collared shirt, and black suit jacket. Charming and suave as only the ginger-haired Saber could be, he sauntered his six-three frame her way.

"Well, if it isn't Teylor Thompson."

Teylor smiled and placed her plate on the counter so she could give him a hug.

"Girl, where've you been all my life?" he asked in his normal smooth tone.

Teylor rolled her eyes. "Saber, it's less than a two hour drive from you to me. You hardly ever come back to Spirit Lake anymore. You've traded us in for Phoenix."

"More honeys in Phoenix," he said with a wink. He directed his next sentence at Rima. "Small town living isn't really my thing. Running into the same women every day gets old."

Rima glared at Saber and said, "Boy, don't play with me. You wouldn't know a real woman if she was staring you in your face. You just crawl into whatever hole'll open for you."

"Is that an invitation?" he asked with a wicked grin.

"Not even in your horniest dreams," she fired back.

He smirked at her.

Another disgusted eye roll came from Rima, and she stomped away saying, "I'm losing my appetite."

"That's damn near impossible with the way she eats," he said, chuckling and focusing his attention back on Teylor.

"Why do you two carry on like that?" she asked him.

"Because she's a scorpion woman."

"You were probably made for each other."

"You know, T, I've always considered you like a sister. Don't make me reconsider."

Teylor burst out in laughter. "You are so crazy."

Saber rarely came around anymore, and even though he and Rima had their issues, Teylor missed having him around.

"So what do you think about the newest addition?" he asked referring to Carrie, his voice barely above a whisper.

"She's nice," Teylor said casually. "He seems to be in love with her."

Saber stole a glance in Carrie's direction. She and Charleston were chatting away. Jamie and Rima were involved in a heavy debate about what song to play next.

"Seems to be," he echoed.

He faced her again. His eyes held compassion, telling her he knew she was hurting. Saber was a little rough around the edges, and to people who didn't know him well, aside from Rima, he could come off as obnoxious, but he cared deeply for his friends. Being the only child of deceased parents and raised by his grandmother, Teylor, Jamie, and even Rima were his family. Like Rima, he also knew that her feelings for Jamie surpassed friendship. Lately it seemed everyone knew. Everyone but Jamie.

Teylor forced a smile and looked away.

"What do you want me to say?" she asked softly.

"Nothing, T."

He put his hand on her shoulder. "Those who love you don't need words. We just know to try and be there."

Teylor looked at Jamie. "If only that were true."

"Give him time. He's a smart man. He'll figure it out, if he hasn't already."

Teylor smiled again, this time genuinely. Saber wrapped her in a friendly hug, just in time for Teylor to lock eyes with Jamie.

Lots of laughter ensued as the night carried on. They debated everything from politics to music and movies. Rima assured Jamie that they would all be in for a boring wedding if he had anything to do with the music choices, adding that maybe Carrie could give them more hope. But when Carrie said that she preferred classical, Rima replied, "LOOORRRD, we're all in trouble."

Everyone laughed and moved into guessing each other's favorite childhood movies. No one could figure out the other's choice until it was time to guess Jamie's. Carrie's eyes lit up with confidence and she shouted out her guess first.

"Back to the Future."

"No," Charleston countered. "He would always watch *Stand by Me*."

"That's *my* favorite, C," Saber corrected.

Teylor watched as they all went back and forth roaring out a host of infamous flicks from the eighties and nineties. Finally she intervened.

"Goonies. It's *The Goonies."*

Silence invaded the room and all eyes went to Jamie, waiting for him to confirm. He looked at Teylor.

"Teylor guessed it. It's *The Goonies."*

Rima threw her hands up in the air. "Of course she knows. They only watch it together every other week."

The awkward air in the room sent blood rushing to Rima's cheeks when she realized what she'd done. Teylor glanced at Carrie, who was already staring back at her, her eyes cool but disgruntled. Teylor quickly looked away. Saber, who'd been watching the quiet exchange came up with an idea of his own.

"Let's play a game."

"Wrong set of friends, Saber. We're not into those kinky shenanigans you're used to," Rima quipped.

"Don't fret, sweetheart. When the time is right, you'll have your turn," he replied coolly.

Rima replied with an ice cold stare.

They all spread out on the sectional, except Carrie, who was snuggled up next to Jamie. Saber opted for a dining chair that he placed directly in front of the couch, facing the others. A sneaky grin settled on his face as he eyed each of his friends.

Jamie asked, "Man, what are you up to?"

Saber faked offense and grabbed his chest. "Is that what you all really think of me? That every time I make a suggestion, I gotta be up to something?"

They all replied "yes" in unison.

Saber looked shocked and then smiled.

"You're right," he confessed, and they all laughed.

"Okay," he said, rubbing his hands together. "Let's take it back to the old school. How about a good old-fashioned game of Truth or Dare?"

"Oh hell no," Rima shouted. "Not with you. I'm not telling you my business."

"What business? You live in a small town and make coffee all day," Saber cracked.

Rima rolled her eyes so hard, Teylor thought they'd pop out of her head.

"Come on, what are you guys so worried about? You're all saints, right? I'm the only heathen here, agreed?"

They all remained quiet.

"Okay, I'll keep it PG-13."

No response.

"Damn, rated G!"

"Saber, we'll play. Go ahead," Charleston said finally, agreeing for everyone.

"Thank you, Sista Charlie," Saber said, mocking like they were in church. Then he dove right in with the questions.

"Jamie," he said turning to face him with a grin. Jamie took a deep breath. "Truth or dare?"

"Truth."

"A man that takes risks. I like that," Saber joked. "If you had to be stuck on an island for ten years, who is the one person you'd want to be with you?"

For anyone else, this might have been an easy question, but because all of the people in the room, aside from Carrie, knew how inseparable Jamie and Teylor had always been, even if he said Carrie, the others knew there was a strong possibility that he was thinking about Teylor.

Before Jamie could get the words out, Carrie spoke. "That's an easy question, right, darling?" she asked, looking at him. "He'd choose his soon-to-be wife."

"Would he?" Saber questioned.

"What do you mean, 'would he'? Of course he would. Who else would he choose?"

Saber gave a knowing shrug.

"There he goes causing trouble," Rima said under her breath.

"Why don't we let the man answer the question," Saber finished.

All eyes were on Jamie. "Well, Jamie," he urged.

"Saber," Jaime warned.

"Jamie, answer the question," Carrie implored.

Saber chimed in. "Remember, you have to live with this person and this person only for ten whole years."

Teylor kept her eyes on Jamie. Even though he was playing it cool, she knew him too well not to know he was a ball of nerves. He glanced at her so quickly that if she'd blinked, she would have missed it. His eyes fell back on Carrie.

"Of course it would be you, babe."

Carrie gave a satisfied smile and kissed his cheek. Jamie looked back at Saber, who was peering at him. Saber raised one eyebrow giving Jamie the indication that he knew he was lying but had decided to let it slide. Saber faced Teylor.

"T, same question."

"Are you kidding me?" Rima blurted out.

"Calm down, Rima," Charleston intervened.

Rima rolled her eyes and shook her head in disgust.

"Saber, don't you have another question you could ask Teylor?" Charleston asked.

Saber looked at Charleston. "Nope." He diverted his attention back to Teylor.

"Same question, T. Ten years. One person."

"Saber, you didn't even give me the choice of truth or dare," Teylor reminded him.

Once again, Rima shook her head in disgust. Saber ignored her and asked Teylor, "Truth or dare, T."

"Dare," she answered, grinning.

"Touché."

He looked around the room for a challenge that would make Teylor change her mind. She saw him eyeing the peach cobbler and knew he remembered how much she hated it, and how she'd almost thrown up after being dared to taste it when they were in college. He smirked, looked at her, and gave his dare.

"Take a bite of that peach cobbler over there."

Teylor's eyes went wide.

"That's the dare," Saber said, chuckling.

Just the thought of taking a bite of the cobbler made Teylor sick to her stomach. There was no way she'd be taking that dare. As much as she didn't want the awkwardness that she knew was going to come with her answer—or the menacing stares from Carrie it would bring— she'd much rather that than vomiting all over Jamie's kitchen. She said her answer softly.

"I'm sorry, I couldn't hear you, T. Could you speak up?"

"Jamie," she said loudly.

"Jamie, what?" Saber asked.

She glared at Saber, refusing to back down. "On the island for ten years…it would be with Jamie."

A grandiose smile rested on Saber's face. Teylor's eyes avoided Carrie's like the plague but somehow they found Jamie's and held an unspoken conversation. Teylor was wordlessly letting him know that she didn't regret her answer. She'd always choose him. He was apologizing because he knew his answer wasn't the one she wanted to hear.

"I'm through with this game," Rima insisted.

"Me too," Charleston agreed.

Content with his mischief, Saber agreed to end the game, stating, "You guys are no fun anyway. If you'd rather sit around and look at each other all night, be my guest."

"It's getting late, I'm gonna head home," Charleston announced.

"It's only ten-thirty, Charlie," Jamie said, glancing at the gold watch around his wrist.

"Yeah I know, but the kids are staying the night at Mom and Dad's and I could use some time to myself before Jonathan gets home." She arose from the couch and started gathering her belongings.

"Where is Jonathan, anyway?" asked Teylor. "I feel like I haven't seen him in forever."

"He's in Phoenix working," she explained. Charleston sighed, allowing the annoyance to filter through her tone. "Always working," she muttered as she made her way to the door.

"I'll walk you to the elevator," Jamie said, following her into the hall outside of his apartment.

"Are you sure you're ready for this, Jamie?" Charlie asked softly the moment they were in the hall.

He closed the front door to give them more privacy.

"For what?"

"Marriage."

Jamie saw the sadness in her eyes and realized that her question had little to do with him.

"What's going on with you and Jonathan, Charleston?"

Jamie's direct question made her freeze. Her eyes watered but she remained quiet.

"You've been different. As much as you try to hide it, I see behind the smiles. I haven't seen you wear your hair down in a while or overly dressed up like you normally are. Lately you seem to just be going through the motions."

She looked away and solemnly hung her head. Jamie gently placed his hand under her chin and lifted her gaze to meet his eyes.

"I know I have my own issues I'm dealing with, but you can talk to me, Charlie. I'm never too busy for you."

She allowed the tears to fall. Jamie tried wiping them away but the more he wiped, the more they came.

"You've always been so attentive." She smiled through the tears. "I see why everyone loves you so much. The boy with the heart as deep as his dimples."

Jamie smiled and embraced her in a hug. It had been a long time since he'd seen her so hurt. If he could, he'd take her pain and make it his own. He hated seeing the people he loved in so much despair.

When they let go, Charleston confided in him.

"I think Jonathan's having an affair," she confessed.

"What? No way."

"Jamie, he's always working. Always. I don't even think he's coming home tonight. He's been staying overnight two, sometimes three times a week."

Jamie shook his head, unable to fathom Charleston's theory. She and Jonathan had been together since high school, and like other couples, they'd seen the worst and the best of times, but Jonathan's love for Charleston had always been evident. Like their parents' marriage, Charleston and Jonathan's relationship was one that Jamie wanted for himself. Jonathan was a successful self-employed accountant while Charleston was a devoted wife and stay-at-home mother. Together they shared two amazing and well-behaved children that were the apple of Jamie's eye. He just couldn't see Jonathan throwing all of that away for a fling. As far as he knew, Jonathan was a man of God and a loving husband and father.

"He's always been a hard worker, Charlie. Have you come right out and asked him?"

"I can't. I don't want to be that insecure woman."

Jamie frowned.

"Insecure? What is it with women and that word? He's your husband, Charlie. You're allowed to feel vulnerable. Your marriage is supposed to be a safe place for the two of you to share everything."

He let out a breath of air.

"One thing women always forget, we can't read your minds. You have to tell us what's going on in that head of yours. Talk to him."

Charleston folded her arms and leaned against the wall. "Yeah, maybe."

"Not maybe, do it. Jonathan's no fool. He wouldn't throw away what he has in you and the kids. In the meantime, I'll be in prayer for both of you, and you let me know if there is anything else I can do."

She smiled and kissed Jamie on the cheek.

"Thanks, little brother. I'm gonna get going."

She turned to leave, but stopped and faced him. "You know, marriage may not be so bad for you after all."

With a wink, she headed toward the elevator.

When Jaime returned inside the apartment, everyone was gathered around the piano laughing and cracking jokes. Saber was attempting to play the keys while singing off tune in a high-pitched voice. Jamie walked over to the piano and said, "Rima, let's save Saber before he hurts himself."

Saber chuckled and moved out of the way to allow Jamie to take his seat. Rima squeezed beside him and whispered in his ear. Jamie nodded and started playing the keys. Right away Teylor knew the song, and Rima gave her a soft smile. Elvis' *Can't Help Falling in Love*. She was singing it for Teylor and Jamie. Rima took a deep breath, closed her eyes, and started singing.

Her voice was steady and hauntingly beautiful. She belted out the lyrics with soul, as if she were singing of her own unrequited love. Teylor stole a glance at Carrie, who was swaying, eyes closed, caught up in her own rapture of the melody. Even Saber was bobbing his head in delight.

Then Rima was singing the last of the lyrics, her voice reaching a higher octave.

Teylor rested her eyes on Jamie. He gave each key his undivided attention, allowing himself to become the music. She loved when he was in this element. So free. The lyrics were saying what she couldn't and all she could do was watch. His eyes were closed and when he opened them, hers were waiting for him.

Maybe she was foolish, but she couldn't help herself. She was in love with her best friend.

TEN

After a full night of tossing and turning, Teylor woke up groggy the next morning. She pulled herself out of bed and headed straight for the shower. She let the hot water cascade down her head and over her face. It almost seemed as if the water was washing away the remnants of the previous night. Thoughts of Jamie plagued her mind, and she kept waking up throughout the night. Feeling like she'd only had an hour of sleep, Teylor stayed in the shower longer than usual, hoping the water would refresh her mind and renew her spirit. When the water started to run cold, she knew it was time to get out. The shower helped to wake her up a bit but it did nothing to distract her from reality.

Teylor made a hot cup of vanilla chai, along with two scrambled eggs and a slice of toast. She hadn't had much of an appetite lately. Rima had mentioned that she seemed to be losing weight, but Teylor hadn't realized it until she slid on her favorite pair of sweats this morning and noticed how loose they were around her waist. The only reason she was eating at all was to keep from shedding any more pounds. After forcing half of the toast and one egg down her throat, Teylor decided she was done. One more bite and she'd hurl.

Despite what was going on in Teylor's world, the day was majestic. It was about eighty-five degrees, and the sun was in a forgiving mood—it shone bright, but wasn't blazing. The trees danced in the light breeze and the lake sparkled like gold treasure. Several people were out fishing and swimming, others picnicked on the bank. All this weekday activity on the lake was a sure sign that summer was in full swing.

Teylor sat on the dock just beyond her cottage. She threw her head back and allowed the sun to toast her skin, her feet oscillating in the cool water. A deep inhale and slow exhale later, Teylor was beginning to feel a lot better. She felt more relaxed. She had nothing figured out with Jamie but peace settled on her mind, assuring her that everything would be alright.

"Thank You, Jesus," she said aloud.

Teylor sat out on the dock for a long while, watching teenagers swim and have playful water fights. Mothers cautiously coddled their small children to keep them from getting too close to the bank's edge. Fisherman sat patiently awaiting their big catch of the day. Spirit Lake was a magical place, and she couldn't imagine herself living anywhere else. It had always been her home and it always would be.

After basking in the sun, Teylor decided to get some writing done and made her way into town to her "second home." Still wearing her favorite charcoal sweats and a pale yellow V-neck T-shirt with black flip-flops, she pulled open the large wooden doors and stepped into the cozy den of books.

The bookstore was a quaint little place that resembled an old library and acted as both. Adel's Books, named for the owner's late wife, was a two-story paradise for book lovers. Old books and wild imaginings flooded her senses, and Teylor couldn't help but smile; the scent always warmed her. Wall-to-wall oak bookcases filled with information and creativity for everyone from children, tweens, teens, and adults sat waiting for those who wanted to go on a literary adventure. Teylor had taken many of her own over the years.

Six wooden tables made a straight line down the center of the store. Each table had an antique brass desk lamp and four wooden chairs. One large window let in rays of sunlight—the rays acted as spotlights throughout the ground floor. A winding staircase leading to the upper floor hid in the corner.

Aside from a group of four teenagers huddling and whispering at one of the tables, the place was empty and peacefully quiet. The owner, Mr. Henry, sat behind his large oak desk at the far end of the bookstore reading a book. He looked up and smiled at Teylor when she walked in. Mr. Henry was eighty years old but still moved around well. He was tall with dark brown skin and bushy white eyebrows that shadowed friendly black eyes. His white hair, like his eyebrows, was thick and curly but thinning in the middle.

He and his wife, Adel, had opened the bookstore long ago, before Teylor was even born. Adel had been an avid reader and lover of books, so as a birthday gift one year, Mr. Henry had surprised her with her very own library. Wanting to share the love of her personal sanctuary with others, Adel convinced her husband to make her library public. Soon after, they began selling and lending out books to the townspeople. After she passed away, Mr. Henry, who was by then retired, refused to close the bookstore and decided to run it himself.

"Adel would come back to life and kill me if I closed this place," he'd say.

He'd hardly changed a thing since she died, including the old-fashioned library cards used to check out books. One of Teylor's favorite parts of borrowing books was the old stamped cards that told a history of like minds with the same interests, some even dating back forty years prior. She'd always spend some time going over the names of previous borrowers before signing her own name and watching Mr. Henry stamp it with a due date.

Once or twice a week, so Mr. Henry could run errands or take a break, Teylor would volunteer to operate the store. They'd become really good friends over the years, and Teylor enjoyed his company. Today she was focused on getting some writing done, however, so she smiled, waved, and pointed to her laptop bag. He nodded his understanding and went back to reading, refusing to bother her when she needed to be writing. He was always encouraging her to get her novel finished. She often felt as if he took her writing more seriously than she did, and figured it had a lot to do with Adel's passion for books.

Teylor took the winding staircase to the second floor, her favorite section of the library. More bookcases covered one wall while the others displayed black and white portraits of African American writers such as W. E. B. DuBois, Frances Harper, Jessie Redmon Fauset, Harriet E. Wilson, Maya Angelou, Langston Hughes, Frederick Douglass, and others. Plush olive green couches paired with small wooden tables covered the burgundy carpeted floor making for a very comfortable and enduring reading space. Much to Teylor's liking, she was the only person on the second floor, so she made herself comfortable on the couch closest to the window and took out her laptop.

Two hours had passed by the time Teylor decided to take a break and stretch. When her stomach growled, she realized she hadn't eaten since breakfast. She left her laptop behind Mr. Henry's desk and walked across the way to Lucy's diner for a salad and biscuits.

Teylor closed her eyes as she bit into one of the warm biscuits. She was famished and the delicious bread hit the spot. It was a little after the lunch rush and the crowd had died down, so she sat in her and Jamie's usual booth. Sandy came over and refilled her glass with sweet iced tea. Teylor smiled, said "thank you," and Sandy whisked away to care for some other customers.

Teylor was downing the last of her tea when she saw Carrie enter the diner. Carrie was as sweet as pie but being in her presence knowing she had every intention of telling her fiancé that she was in love with him didn't sit right with Teylor's conscience. Her eyes darted toward the back door and just when she was about to make a dash for it, she and Carrie made eye contact. Carrie smiled and hurried toward her.

Hair immaculate, draped over one shoulder, black silk, thigh length dress and black wedges made Carrie a sight for sore eyes, but for Teylor, it had the opposite effect. She forced a smile and waved.

"Were you leaving?" Carrie asked when she made it to Teylor's table.

"Actually, yes. I'm doing some writing over at the bookstore and just needed a lunch break," she said, gesturing at the empty plates on the table.

Ignoring Teylor's response, Carrie sat down across from her. She placed her black leather bag beside her and put her hand in the air to grab Sandy's attention. Sandy's eyes said what Teylor was thinking: *What in the world is going on here?* She approached cautiously, her eyes bouncing from Teylor to Carrie. Finally she asked, "Hi there, how can I help you?"

"Hello, Sandy. Can I please have an iced tea, no sugar, and a house salad? Hold the croutons and dressing on the side."

Sandy gave her an odd look. "Is that it?"

"That will be all, thank you," Carrie answered with a smile.

After Sandy left to fill the order, Carrie stared at Teylor without saying a word. Teylor cleared her throat and shifted in her seat.

"So, how are you liking Spirit Lake?" she finally asked.

"Very beautiful."

More awkward silence.

"Where's Jamie? Thought you two would be spending some time together today."

"No, he's working."

Sandy returned with the order and hurried away, but not before giving Teylor a look of warning. Carrie picked at a piece of lettuce.

"This is your and Jamie's place of meeting, correct?"

"Our place of meeting?" Teylor asked, unsure of where the conversation was heading.

"The two of you meet here weekly for lunch?"

"Oh, um, yeah. Just for lunch."

"And this is the booth you two share?"

Teylor was hesitant to answer. She had a feeling in the pit of her stomach that this wasn't going to end well.

"It's my favorite. I like to look out at the bookstore." She pointed out the window. Carrie didn't bother to look. Her lips were curved into a superficial smile, and her eyes were steady on Teylor.

"You're set to meet tomorrow, correct?"

Teylor's patience was wearing thin. Carrie was asking too many questions, and Teylor wasn't sure where she was going with the interrogation. She was over it already. Forcing a smile, she answered, "You're welcome to join us."

Carrie let out a curt chuckle. "No thanks. I don't really care for the food."

Lies, Teylor thought. At the fellowship picnic, Carrie had been eating Ms. Lucy's chicken and potato salad like a starving animal. She wondered what had changed, but decided to keep her thoughts to herself. Growing tired of the interview, and unwilling to try and change the subject to engage in small talk, Teylor decided it was time to leave.

"Well, I should be getting back to the bookstore. I have a lot of work still to do, and I left my laptop there."

She began to stand when Carrie's parting words gave her pause. She wasn't sure she'd heard her right.

"Excuse me?"

"I said, you're in love with him."

Teylor's heart sank to the pit of her stomach. Her eyes traveled to the entrance and then back to Carrie.

"Have a seat, Teylor," she said, gesturing toward the other side of the booth. "Please. I won't take up too much of your time. I promise."

Teylor hesitated for a moment, once again eyeing the exit. Knowing she'd have to either face it or risk being outed to Jamie, she reluctantly sat down.

"You are in love with him, aren't you?"

Teylor thought she'd shrivel up and die, but forced herself to remain calm. She cleared her throat. "In love with who?" she asked.

A half smile covered Carrie's face. One that said she wasn't the slightest bit amused with Teylor's phony naiveté.

"Jamie," she responded plainly.

Teylor's face scrunched up and she forced a laugh. Suddenly she knew there was no way she could have this conversation with Carrie when she hadn't even told Jamie how she truly felt.

"Carrie, I—"

"Teylor, please," she said, interrupting. Carrie's voice was soft but authoritative. "Men are different," she continued. "Either they pretend not to see, or they choose not to see, but women…women are extremely intuitive."

She paused and waited for Teylor to admit it, but Teylor wasn't budging.

"Look, Carrie, we're friends—have been for a long time. I can see how you might think that but…"

"At first I asked myself if it was me. Am I making the matter more than what it is? But, no. You make it more obvious than you probably intend to."

Teylor's words caught in her throat, and she tried clearing it again. Carrie was peering at her so intensely, Teylor was sure the other woman could see right through to her soul. But she didn't want Jamie to find out this way. Not from Carrie. Teylor had her defense ready, but found it hard to deliver. She looked at Carrie again. Her eyes were knowing, and Teylor was sure there was a little fear in them. She couldn't deny her feelings even if she wanted to, but strangely enough, a part of her didn't want to deny it at all. If Carrie told Jamie, then so be it. They'd both have found out eventually.

Teylor dropped her eyes and said, "What do you want me to say?"

Carrie's face settled, relief sweeping over her as if she'd been trying to prove that she wasn't imagining things.

"There's nothing to say," she answered. "I can't blame you."

Teylor met her eyes again.

"Who could? He's so loving toward you, so mindful of your heart."

Another pause.

"I've even wondered if he's in love with you also, but according to him, his feelings for you are no more than a sibling's affection. Similar to his and Charleston's relationship."

A lump formed in Teylor's throat. She swallowed hard to force it back down. Hearing Jamie loved her like a sister was threatening to make her spill her lunch. All hope of them being anything more than friends was slowly diminishing. She took a deep breath to calm her nerves. Carrie was silently studying her. The tiniest smirk appeared on her face. Teylor needed to leave, but Carrie wasn't finished.

"I realize how difficult this must be for you, knowing that the man you love is in love with another woman, but the fact is, Teylor, I love him too. We're getting married."

Teylor gave her eyes a soft roll—the lump was making its way back up her throat.

"I, uh...think I should excuse myself," she choked out.

Ignoring her, Carrie continued. "I'm not sure if he's mentioned it to you, but we've advanced our wedding date."

Teylor's eyes widened but she couldn't speak. Suddenly, beads of sweat started forming at her hairline; her stomach felt like a raging sea.

"From the look on your face, I gather that you were unaware. Well, the new date is set for a week from Saturday. You may want to..."

A low moan escaped from Teylor's throat. She could no longer hear what Carrie was saying. How could Jamie do this to her, without even telling her? Whatever strength she had left in her was gone. She was going to vomit. Teylor bolted to the bathroom and let it all out. Afterward, she cried.

ELEVEN

Teylor rinsed her mouth and pressed a cool, wet paper towel to her face. She repeatedly inhaled and exhaled in order to calm herself and stop the tears. Just when she had finally regained her composure, Ms. Lucy came bursting through the restroom door, startling her.

"Teylor, are you alright?" she asked frantically. "Sandy said you ran in here like you were gonna be sick or somethin'."

She grabbed Teylor's face in her palms, checked for fever by feeling her forehead, and asked if she needed a doctor.

"I'm fine, Ms. Lucy."

"Well, are you sure?"

She felt Teylor's forehead again and started checking her pulse. Teylor gently took her hands and placed them in her own.

"Ms. Lucy, I'm okay. I promise," she responded, reassuring her.

With worry etched on her face, Ms. Lucy looked at Teylor's puffy red eyes.

"You don't look okay, honey. You've been crying. Why? Looks like you've been throwing up too."

Teylor closed her eyes and took a deep breath.

The older woman frowned. "This wouldn't have anything to do with Ms. Thang out there, would it?" She grabbed Teylor's chin like a mother disciplining her young. "Look at me, child."

Teylor's eyes snapped open and filled with tears. She had all the respect in the world for Ms. Lucy but she was simply too exhausted to talk about what had just transpired. She slouched against the tiled wall, sniffling.

"Girl, you look wore out. How did you ever let anybody get you to this point?"

Teylor hung her head. She'd been asking herself that question for the past week, but still she had no answers.

"I guess love will do that to you, huh?"

"Ms. Lucy, forgive me, but I don't have the energy to talk about it."

"Well, don't talk, just listen. I've been watching you and Jamie come in here every week since y'all were teenagers. Every week, y'all sit at that same booth talking, laughing, and carrying on."

Teylor grabbed another paper towel from the dispenser and wiped her eyes. "We're friends, Ms. Lucy."

"Yeah, I know, but it always looked like more than that to me."

Teylor peered at Ms. Lucy. "What do you mean?"

"I've only seen that look—the way you two look at each other— a couple of times in my life. It's love, Teylor, and not just any kind of love. It's the kind of love that God joins together."

"He's getting married, Ms. Lucy."

"Hell, I know that and so what. He's not married yet, is he?"

"What do you suggest I do? I'm not the one he's in love with."

Ms. Lucy's brows furrowed together. "What he has with that woman ain't love, child," she answered, swatting her hand in the air as if she was trying to kill a gnat. She grabbed Teylor's face with the palms of her hands and looked into her eyes. Her smile was sympathetic. "You already know what you need to do."

And Teylor did know. She needed to do what Rima had been telling her to do all along. She needed to tell him, and if Ms. Lucy was right when she said that God had joined them together, then maybe her chances were better than she perceived them to be.

Ms. Lucy hugged her tightly and started for the door.

"Ms. Lucy? Why didn't you end up with either of them?"

"With who, dear?"

"Those men, who looked at you like God had joined you together?"

"Child, no man has ever looked at me that way. I wish he had though," she said with a chuckle. "Nah, I haven't been blessed in that way, but Mr. Henry and Adel; they shared that blessing. And Jamie's seen it his whole life with Edward and Gail. Yeah, they still have something special. It'd been a long time since I'd seen love like that, then you and Jamie came along. Believe me when I tell you it's real. Most people go their whole lives looking for it and never find it. You have it. Don't let it pass you by."

~

That night Teylor lay in bed, snuggled beneath the covers. Lately all she seemed to be doing was trying to forget. Forget the ball of mess her life had become. Teylor felt exhausted and utterly defeated. Her mother would be so disappointed. Unlike Teylor, she'd been a fighter, fighting all the way to the end of her life.

Teylor tried to force sleep, but it was of no use. The night was still young, and she couldn't escape thoughts of Carrie, wondering if she'd revealed to Jamie how Teylor really felt about him, and if she had, was it the end of their friendship? Teylor flipped over on her stomach and pulled the down comforter over her head. Squeezing her eyes shut, she gave slumber another try. Fail. Her hands searched beneath the covers for the remote control. If sleep wouldn't distract her, television would. Still fumbling under the covers, she grasped something cold and hard, and when it started buzzing in her hand, she realized it was her cell phone.

Teylor's heart skipped a beat when she glanced at the glowing screen.

Jamie was calling.

Carrie had told him.

She placed the phone down and stared at the ceiling until the buzzing stopped, courage deserting her yet again. She couldn't talk to him now. Plain and simple, she was scared. Teylor took slow even breaths, forcing herself not to lose it. A moment later, the buzzing began again. This time it was a text message.

Hey T. You're going to voicemail. Are we still on for lunch tomorrow?

She sighed with relief after reading his message. Maybe he was still in the dark, and her secret was safe. Still, she wasn't ready to face him, and there was no guarantee that Carrie wouldn't accompany him. Things were going to be different from here on out. Teylor made a promise to herself. The next time she saw Jaime, he'd know the truth and she'd be the one to deliver it. In the meantime, she needed an excuse as to why she couldn't make it to lunch. She decided to use the oldest one in the book. Not wanting him to know she'd purposely ignored his call, she waited five minutes before replying.

Sorry, Jamie, I'm not feeling well.

His reply came immediately.

What's going on? You need me to bring you something? Soup?

Teylor smiled. Carrie was right. He was very loving toward her—always available when she needed him. She decided to be more personal, hoping he'd shy away and let her off the hook.

Teylor: *No. Women's stuff.*

Jamie: *Midol? Heating pad?*

Teylor laughed out loud. She didn't know why she'd ever thought that would work for him. While most men wanted nothing to do with women when it came to the dreaded time-of-the-month, Jamie wasn't intimidated. He'd brought her Midol and a heating pad before, once when she was bent over in agony from period cramps. When she'd asked if he was uncomfortable, he'd said, "My mom made me go to the store and buy tampons for my sister once. Said if I planned on having a wife and maybe a daughter, I'd better get used to it. This is me getting used to it."

Teylor: *I guess you finally got used to it.*

Jamie: [wink face emoji] *No worries about tomorrow. Rest up. Let me know if you need anything.*

Teylor: *The best friend a girl could ever ask for.*

Jamie: *I do what I can, lol.*

Teylor: *Night*

Jamie: *Night, Mahogany.*

For Teylor, sleep came peacefully.

~

Jamie wallowed in the crisp night air, sipping wine as he took in the view. From his terrace, the town lights let off a soft glow, leaving the moon and stars to do their job. They were shining bright this evening, and Jamie silently thanked God for such a glorious sight. Summer nights were his favorite, and tonight he was sharing it with the woman he loved.

He and Carrie basked in the candlelight beneath the stars on his balcony—chicken Alfredo filled their bowls; red wine, their glasses. He gazed into her beautiful dark brown eyes and smiled.

"You have the most alluring smile, Jameson."

Jamie chuckled. "Jameson? You're calling me by my full government, now?"

A half smile crossed her face. "I'm partial to Jameson. Everyone calls you Jamie. I want something for myself."

"How about 'husband'?"

Her half smile morphed into a full grin. "Perfect," she said, raising her glass for a toast. "To us."

Jamie raised his glass and repeated, "To us."

They ate in silence, enjoying each other's company. Jamie watched as Carrie gracefully held her knife and fork, carefully cutting each piece into smaller ones and taking tiny bites. He laughed inwardly. She emanated elegance—every move she made was precise and calculated. There had been many times when he'd wanted to tell her to relax, just go with the flow, but maybe this was her flow. They were different in many ways. She delighted in classical music; he preferred R&B. She was a clean eater while carbs were his forte. He wondered how they'd managed to fall in love, recalling Teylor's comparison of Paris and Spirit Lake. Maybe she had a point. Regardless, Carrie was the woman he was going to marry, and he was willing to accept their differences.

"Are you and Teylor having your weekly lunch date tomorrow?"

He shook his head. "She's not feeling well."

"That's unfortunate," she murmured before taking another minuscule bite. A strained silence descended before she asked her next question.

"Will this continue after the wedding?"

Jamie paused and looked at her. "Does it bother you?"

"It was just a question, Jameson."

"Okay, so answer mine."

She kept quiet, pushing food around her plate.

"Carrie. Look at me."

Her eyes complied.

"If we're going to be married, we need to be honest with each other."

She gently placed her fork in her plate and wiped the corners of her mouth with a dinner napkin. Then she looked him straight in the eye.

"I don't know, Jamie. I guess I need to know how this works."

"How *what* works?"

"I'm going to be the most important woman in your life, or at least I should be."

"You already are."

"So how does this work? How does having a female best friend and a wife function? How do you balance the two without offending one?"

That was the question Jamie had been trying to figure out since they became engaged. He was already worn down from trying to figure out Teylor's issue while keeping their relationship intact. He didn't have the vigor to shelter both women indefinitely. It was all becoming too much to bear. One relationship would eventually falter.

"Carrie—"

"Answer something for me, Jamie," she interrupted. "Your interactions with Teylor...are they...strictly platonic?"

Jamie's eyes opened wide and then narrowed into slits. He couldn't believe what he was hearing. He gripped the stem of the wineglass as thoughts about what prompted such a question hurtled through his mind. He knew more than anyone how close he and Teylor were, but he'd never given Carrie any reason to believe he was unfaithful to her—especially with his own best friend, whom he had been so excited to introduce her to. What kind of man did she take him for?

Suddenly, any hope of the three of them being tight vanished. She would never see Teylor the way he did, nor did he think Teylor would draw close to Carrie. There would always be a war for his attention. He suddenly felt foolish for thinking he could love two women differently and make everyone happy.

Jamie let out an exasperated breath. "Of course. Teylor and I have—and have always had—a strictly platonic relationship."

Carrie backed down and became quiet when she heard the irritation in his voice. Jamie, regretting his snippy reply, reached out and took her hand. He rubbed the large diamond on her left ring finger.

"You see this?" he asked pointedly. "This is a symbol of my love for you, and only you. The Bible says that a man's wife comes second in his life after God. That's your place." He paused. "Whatever you're not comfortable with, I'll put an end to."

Carrie's eyes sparkled as she leaned in and kissed him on the lips. Jamie welcomed her kiss, but inside he was dying, because he now understood that his new life with Carrie meant ending his old life with Teylor.

~

The next morning brought clear skies and moderate temperatures. The day spoke of new mercies and endless opportunities, but Jamie wasn't feeling optimistic. He woke up and went into prayer, asking God for instructions and wisdom. He had yet to get a response but his faith was firm. God worked at His own pace, and Jamie was certain his prayers would be answered, still the waiting gnawed at his soul.

He stood at the large window in his bedroom, looking over the treetops to where the lake gleamed in the distance. With his mind racing and his heart heavy, he couldn't shake the unease left by his conversation with Carrie last night. She'd made it clear that she didn't want his relationship with Teylor to continue. As his wife-to-be, Carrie's feelings took precedence, but he'd be lying to himself if he said it wasn't tearing him apart to let Teylor go. They'd been through so much together, including the death of her mother and the death of his unborn child. That was the reason for the pact—the abortion. He thought back to those times before he'd surrendered his life to Christ.

During his college years, being away from home had brought out his wild side. He'd begun sleeping around and partying almost immediately, and soon his social life wasn't limited to the weekends. If it hadn't been for Teylor pounding on his dorm-room door every morning and forcing him to class, he would have never graduated. Even when she had to leave school to care for her mother, she'd been at his door bright and early with coffee, muffins, and a smile.

A few years after they'd graduated, a girl Jamie had been casually sleeping with became pregnant with his child, and because they weren't in a serious relationship and, as she put it, she refused to be a single mother on government assistance, she aborted the baby over his protests. Everything halted in Jamie's life. He fell into a depression, and nobody could reach him—except Teylor. She was the only person he would confide in. He told her everything because he knew she was the only person who wouldn't judge him. And she hadn't. She'd been patient with him and supportive, twice a week driving him to a psychologist an hour outside of town so no one would find out his secret; sitting with him for hours at a time, watching movies or playing cards. Sometimes, she would just be there saying nothing. There were many times when he would cry, the guilt of fornication and abortion gnawing at him. Teylor was always there to hold him and read him Scriptures. He still couldn't fathom how she'd been able to nurture him back to sanity and care for her failing mother simultaneously. After some of the hurt subsided, they'd both rededicated their lives to Christ and made a pact to never again have sex before marriage.

Jamie and Teylor were bound to one another through triumph and tragedy, and now Carrie was asking him to cut the ties. How could he sever the strongest bond he'd ever had in his life? The thought made him nauseous, but he now knew that if he was going to have a successful marriage, it was necessary.

He stared past the trees and focused on the lake that held so many cherished memories. Spirit Lake. It was time to say goodbye to the town he adored and hello to the new city he'd fallen in love with. Spirit Lake was his past; Paris was his future.

TWELVE

Teylor's mom sat in the dove-white rocking chair in front of the window in Teylor's room. Quietly, with her hands folded in her lap, she rocked and watched Teylor with adoration in her soft brown eyes, her lips turned up at the corners. Her cinnamon hair hung loosely to her shoulders, and her white dress flowed to the ash-gray wood floor. Teylor sat up in bed and rubbed her eyes. Her heart leapt in her chest when her vision cleared.

"Mommy!"

She jumped out of bed, ran to her mother, and smothered her in a tight hug, refusing to let go. She smelled of fresh flowers on a warm spring day, and Teylor relished in it. It had been so long since she'd held her mom. Tears rained from her eyes, and when her mother wrapped her arms around her, she squeezed tighter.

"Oh, Mommy, I can't believe you're here. I miss you so much," she cried. "Things have gotten so out of control, and I don't know what to do. I can't handle it. I need you." Teylor's despair poured out of her, and she clung to her mother, searching for hope, as if she were the only answer.

"Oh, Teylor, my sweet baby girl." Her mother ran her fingers through Teylor's hair, gently massaging her head. "This is nothing you can't handle. You've always been stronger than you ever believed you were."

Teylor met her mother's doting gaze. "It seems like I'm losing everyone, Mommy. I'm so alone."

Her mother's smile warmed her. "You've never been alone. And you never will be. He will never leave nor forsake you. Look to Him and allow Him to lead you." With tears in her eyes, Teylor's mother said her final words. "I'm so proud of you."

Teylor opened her eyes to the soft light filtering in from the window, her focus immediately on the empty rocking chair. Her leather bound Bible sat where her mother had been in the dream. She wrapped herself in a blanket, walked over to the chair, picked up the holy book, and held it to her chest. Sitting in the rocking chair, Teylor opened the Bible and gasped when she read the highlighted Scripture:

Deuteronomy 31:8: The Lord Himself goes before you and will be with you; He will never leave you nor forsake you. Do not be afraid; do not be discouraged.

Teylor felt all the blood drain from her head as her shoulders shook uncontrollably—tears spilled forth like water from a dam. Emotions ran through her like an Olympic sprinter. Anger, sadness, uncertainty, relief, and joy all threatened to tear her down. She allowed each to have its turn. Snuggling in the rocking chair like a newborn child and hugging her Bible, Teylor awaited rebirth.

~

"So your parents just up and decided to fly in today?"

Jamie and Carrie were halfway to Phoenix in route to Sky Harbor airport.

"Well, they didn't want to miss the engagement party your parents are hosting for us tomorrow."

"I thought they'd decided to come down next week, a few days before the ceremony."

Carrie shrugged carelessly. "They changed their minds."

She concentrated on the checklist in her lap. Although their nuptials in Spirit Lake would be only a small ceremony, true to her nature, Carrie was carefully planning every detail. She drummed the pen between her fingers.

"Jameson, did Gail contact all the guests for tomorrow?"

"I'm assuming so; my mom's good like that."

"Can you confirm?" Jamie eyed her. "Please," she added with a smile.

He chuckled and shook his head. "Sure, sweetheart."

He took her hand and threaded his fingers between hers. "Babe, I need you to relax. Everything will work out the way it's supposed to."

"I know."

An eerie silence settled between them, and Jamie glanced over to find Carrie staring out of the window, a prisoner to her thoughts. A gentle squeeze of her hand freed her attention. "Something on your mind?"

She licked her lips and fiddled with the diamond stud in her right lobe—something she did when she was carefully choosing her words.

"When are you planning to talk to Teylor?"

His chest rose as he took in the air and deflated upon exhale. He kept his eyes on the winding road as they passed dry desert and mountains laden with cacti. The heat permeated the car more insistently the farther south they drove, and Jamie adjusted the air-conditioning accordingly.

"I know how difficult it is for you to have to do this, Jamie, but...I'll feel more comfortable entering a marriage without baggage."

Baggage. Jamie winced at the word. Teylor was anything but. She'd been a comfort during his darkest hour, a ray of sunshine throughout his life, and he'd been the same for her. He couldn't bear to see the pain in her face when he told her they could no longer be friends. He'd always protected her heart, and now Carrie was asking him to shatter it.

He loved Carrie, but he also loved Teylor, just differently. He loved her in a way he couldn't explain, mainly because he'd never had to. The two of them had always known their value in the other's life, but now things were changing. He'd been forced to define their relationship, and lately, trying to do so seemed to be occupying his every waking moment.

"I hear you, Carrie."

"You hear me but you're not giving me any answers," she said brusquely.

Jamie quickly maneuvered the car to the right lane and exited the highway, barely missing another vehicle. The angry driver sounded his horn as he sped by.

Carrie gripped the dashboard and steadied herself. "Jamie, what are you doing?"

Not bothering to give her an answer, Jamie parked on the shoulder of the road and turned his upper body to face her. She stared at him wide eyed, bottom lip trembling. When Jamie spoke, he kept his voice low but stern.

"Look, Carrie, I love you and I have every intention of giving you and this marriage my all, but don't ever think you can intimidate me with your tone because I'm not acting as fast as you want me to. I told you I would handle it and I will."

Stunned into silence, Carrie's eyes blinked rapidly. "I...I'm sorry," she responded with a quavering voice. "I just want everything to be perfect."

That he knew. She wanted everything perfect, including him, but that was something he wasn't able to give her, and he needed her to understand that before he made her his wife.

"Things will never be perfect, Carrie, but that's the beauty of all this. Two imperfect people loving each other in spite of." He brought her knuckles to his lips. "I need you to relax. Please. For the both of us."

Her smile told him she would try, and for now, that was enough. One battle down, but tomorrow would be a more challenging fight. Tomorrow, he'd face Teylor.

~

Teylor ended the call with Mrs. Westbrook. She'd been invited to Jamie and Carrie's engagement party tomorrow night, and even though she was racked with nerves about encountering them again, she was ready. Well, almost ready. She went to her closet and searched for the right dress.

Still in its plastic cover, the black high-neck, low-back dress had never been worn. Rima had insisted she buy it last spring as a just-in-case. Teylor was glad she'd listened. She stood in front of the mirror and held the knee-length dress against her body. She couldn't remember the last time she'd dressed up, and the reflection in the mirror brought a genuine smile to her lips. For the first time in a while, her outlook was positive. She still didn't know what the future held, but strength was radiating within her, and she knew that tomorrow would be the night. She would tell Jamie everything.

Teylor chose a pair of onyx five-inch stilettos and gold jewelry to accentuate her dress, making sure she'd cause a few gasps and head-turns. Pleased with her choices and with a new pep in her step, she headed to the bathroom to wash her hair.

~

The sun hung low in the western sky, casting off hues of purple, orange, and pink. The air was warm with a cool breeze—not a cloud in the sky. It was a beautiful night for a party—God had been merciful. Jamie and Carrie pulled into the driveway of the Westbrooks' home. The sound of music flooded from the backyard when Jamie killed the engine.

"Looks like they've started without us," he said.

"The party doesn't begin until we arrive, dear," Carrie sassed.

They exited the vehicle and walked the paved pathway toward the backyard. Jamie glanced around at the cars parked on the street before ducking behind the gate. No Teylor. He knew his mom had invited her but he wondered if she'd come. A soft gasp escaped Carrie's lips as they made their way around the house to the backyard. Even Jamie was overwhelmed by the sight. The blanket of grass that spread across the entire yard was freshly cut. The large northern red oak trees were mesmerizing with bone white lanterns hanging from their branches. In between the trees sat an extended dining table and chairs. The table was covered in neutral linens and lined with vases filled with vibrant blooms and succulents. To the far right, another long table was laden with fine china and silverware, dinner napkins, delectable eats, irresistible desserts, and refreshing drinks. Smooth R&B flowed through the outdoor surround sound speakers and the concrete slab that usually housed his parents' patio furniture was now empty. Soft white lights were strung above it, and Jamie guessed it was the makeshift dance floor.

"Well, lookie here, the happy couple has arrived." Edward Westbrook gave his son a strong hug and kissed Carrie on the cheek.

"Carrie, dear, you look stunning."

Carrie did a playful spin in her black chiffon, long sleeve, one-shoulder mini-dress. "Why thank you, Mr. Westbrook," she replied coyly.

"Jamie, you're looking like your old man in that fitted suit. Can't go wrong with black on black. Almost as handsome as me," he teased.

Jamie laughed, popped his collar, and said, "You wish you looked this good, old man."

Jamie was a younger image of his father, save the dimples. Mr. Westbrook, with his bald head and smoke-colored beard was handsome and distinguished.

"Boy, where do you think you get it from? If the good Lord shows you some favor, you may look this good when you get my age," he quipped.

They all laughed and walked over to join the rest of the party.

Everyone who was anyone to Jamie was present. His parents, Charlie and the kids—although Jonathan was still nowhere to be seen—Carrie's parents; Ms. Lucy, who was catering the event; Rima; Saber; and Pastor Nelson, who'd been close friends with his father since Jamie could remember. Seeing them so elegantly dressed with excitement written all over their faces brought a huge grin to Jamie's lips, but the absence of Teylor threatened to cast out his happiness. Still, this was a time to celebrate, and so he would.

The guests greeted the couple with hugs, laughs, and more congratulations, and Jamie started to feel better as the conversations began and the party got underway. He almost felt relieved that Teylor hadn't showed up. It would save him from having to do what he was dreading. Maybe it was a blessing in disguise.

~

Night had fallen by the time Teylor made it to town and found a parking spot two houses down from the Westbrooks' home. Her stomach was doing flips like a gymnast at the summer Olympics, and she stalled before getting out of the car. When she finally managed to force her legs forward, she tried holding her head high to drown out her nerves. Her curly hair swayed against her back. It was the first time she'd worn it down in weeks. The familiar touch felt good against her bare skin. Her gold bangles clinked together as she strutted up the sidewalk and took the paved pathway to the backyard. Sounds of laughter poured out from behind the gate, and Teylor paused. She took a deep breath.

"I can do this…I can do this," she chanted.

Then she rubbed her ruby red lips together, sucked in a breath, and pushed the gate open.

THIRTEEN

When she came in view of the partygoers, all chatter ceased. Everyone stared at her, eyes wide and mouths agape. Teylor stood frozen, wanting to take off running in the other direction, until she realized that though their faces held shock, approval lingered in their gazes. Feeling empowered, she mustered up the courage to speak.

"Good evening, everyone."

A few hellos and head nods was her response. She especially paid attention to Jamie, wanting to see his reaction to her glam look. His eyes held something different than the others', but Teylor couldn't call it. She'd get a chance later to ask his opinion. Gail jumped from her seat, her sleeveless, fuchsia, floor length dress flowing behind her, and went to wrap Teylor in a hug.

"You sure know how to enter a party," she whispered in her ear before pulling away.

Teylor's cheeks flushed, and she couldn't stop the grin that lit up her face. Gail held Teylor's hands and took a step back.

"Look at you. You've always been a gorgeous girl, but tonight is your night. You're breathtaking."

"Thank you," Teylor said in a soft voice, her cheeks almost the same shade as Mrs. Westbrook's gown.

"Come, let's get you something to eat."

Gail led Teylor to the food table. Once she was done loading her plate, she exchanged greetings with the familiar faces, and Mrs. Westbrook introduced her to Carrie's parents. Mrs. King was polite but didn't overextend herself. Teylor got the feeling she was used to people going out of their way for her, not the other way around. And it was easy to see why. Mrs. King had flawless coffee-colored skin, dark downturned eyes, and wide pouty lips. Her makeup was flawless, and she gave off the same modelesque air as her daughter. She gave Teylor a once-over before finally extending her hand.

Mr. King, however, was a bit more accepting. He stood from his seat, unlike his wife, and extended his hand right away, greeting Teylor with a huge grin and a "very nice to meet you." Teylor responded in kind, and Gail waved her to an empty seat between Saber and Rima.

"So, Jameson, Carrie tells me you've been here in this town your entire life. Do you two have any plans to relocate once you're married?" Mrs. King asked.

Teylor listened anxiously but continued eating her meal so as to not give herself away.

"Well, Mrs. Kin—"

"Please, Jameson, call me Debra," she interjected smoothly.

"Sure, Debra, but only if you promise to call me Jamie."

Mrs. King peered over her wineglass at Jamie. "You prefer Jamie over Jameson?"

Teylor softly rolled her eyes. *When Paris meets Spirit Lake*, she thought.

"Mother," Carrie warned.

"What, darling? It's a simple question. I'm not offending you am I, dear?" she asked, looking at Jamie.

He smiled. "I don't mind either name, but all of my close friends call me Jamie," he answered.

"So then you don't mind me calling you Jameson? It's just that I have never understood the reason for nicknames. I find your given name more suitable."

"Mother. Please," Carrie cautioned.

Jamie smirked behind his wineglass. Teylor could tell he was irritated. He always smiled to mask his annoyance. Saber shot her a quick glance and slowly shook his head. He was just as bothered as she and Jamie were.

"Jameson is fine," he said coolly.

Carrie tried to find more neutral ground. "Mother, Jamie and I have yet to make a final decision as to what our living arrangements will be. We may keep his condo here and buy another apartment in Manhattan. My place only has one bedroom, and we'd need more room."

"And you can afford that, Jameson?"

All eyes shot to Teylor as she nearly choked on her food. Rima patted her back, and Saber handed her a glass of water. She took a sip while holding her hand in the air, signaling that she was fine.

"Mrs. King—" Jamie's mother started.

"Debra," Mrs. King insisted.

"Debra," Gail echoed, with a hint of aggravation in her voice. "Jamie makes a great living, and he's smart with money. Whether he can afford it or not is not the issue, and it's most certainly not your issue, my issue, nor anyone else's issue."

Before Debra could respond and things got heated, Mr. King intervened. "This food is delicious. Gail, did you make this?"

"No, I did," Ms. Lucy said flatly, approaching the table with more dinner rolls in hand. She placed them in the center of the table and stood behind Gail with her hands on her hips.

Teylor could see in Ms. Lucy's eyes that she didn't care for the Kings. She was waiting like a guard dog to pounce on anyone who had anything offensive to say about her food.

Mr. King cleared his throat.

"Well, you did a fine job, Ms. uh—"

"Lucy, Daddy. It's Ms. Lucy. She owns the diner in town, remember?"

Ms. Lucy rolled her eyes and walked away mumbling, not caring who noticed.

"So how do you fit into this equation?"

Teylor was busy eating her food and didn't realize she was being addressed.

"Is it Tiffany?"

Teylor looked up and eyed Debra. No correction from Carrie this time, only a blank stare.

Teylor wiped the corners of her mouth with her dinner napkin. "It's Teylor," she responded with a half-smile.

Debra gave her another once-over. "Oh yes, of course."

"I've known Jamie since junior high."

"Oh, I see. Are you an ex fling or something?"

The gall of this woman. Teylor almost flipped her lid, but before she could respond, Jamie interceded on her behalf.

"Debra, she's my friend."

"Just a friend?" she asked, still eyeing Teylor.

"Best friend," Rima announced, her voiced pitched a little higher than normal. Teylor could see her growing frustration with Mrs. King as well.

Debra looked at Rima as if she were an extraterrestrial that just appeared out of thin air.

"And who are you again?"

Rima took a deep breath and glanced at Teylor. Rima had many sides to her. She was intelligent, business savvy, and as sweet as cherry pie, but she was also a spitfire and low on patience when she was provoked. The latter side was rising by the second. Teylor's eyes warned her friend not to take it there, but Rima's eyes said that she was going for it. And she did.

"Look, Debra. I'm Rima, this is Teylor," she said, pointing at herself and then Teylor. "Saber is the red-haired fellow sitting to her right, and we're all friends. Teylor and Jamie have been inseparable since junior high—Saber and I joined the duo during college."

She pointed at Ms. Lucy, who was busy at the food table. "Ms. Lucy over there owns the diner that has the best food west of the Rio Grande; Pastor Nelson's title is self-explanatory, but just in case it goes over your head, he's the pastor of our local church. I'm sure you haven't forgotten your hosts for the evening, Edward and Gail, Jamie's parents. Charlie, Jamie's sister as you know, and her adorable little kiddos are right there, and please tell me you haven't forgotten about Jamie, because if so, I'm gonna be a little more than worried and make a strong suggestion that he rethink this whole marriage thing." Breaking into a large, phony grin, she finished, "And there you have it. We're all one big old happy Spirit Lake family. Any questions?"

Debra's eyes were wide, and she let out an exasperated, "Well!"

Carrie's frown showed her distaste for Rima's rant, and everyone else was stunned into silence—everyone except for Saber, who couldn't help but let out a small chuckle.

Carrie glared at Rima and said, "I see that some of us lack manners. This is no way to conduct oneself at a dinner party."

"Right? You'd think she'd know better," Rima fired back, nodding at Debra.

Carrie's mouth fell open slightly, and Mrs. King was visibly on the verge of exploding when Al Green came to the rescue. *Let's Stay Together* started blaring through the speakers, which prompted Mr. King to grab his wife by the hand.

"This is our favorite song, sweetheart."

"This is *your* favorite song," she corrected, still glaring at Rima. "You know I'm not fond of this genre of music."

He hid his embarrassment with a smile. "Well, dance with me anyway, darling."

Finally, Debra removed her focus from Rima. Throwing her dinner napkin on the table, she agreed snippily. "Oh alright."

"Jamie, let's dance," Carrie insisted. "It's a little crowded at this table."

Rima rolled her eyes and headed to the beverage table to pour herself a glass of wine, and Saber followed. Once Jamie and Carrie joined the Kings on the dance floor, Gail began to vent her distaste for Debra.

"The nerve of that woman," she said, facing her husband but speaking loud enough for the rest of the table to hear. " 'You know I'm not fond of this genre of music,' " she parroted in a mocking tone. "Who in the hell does that woman think she is?"

"That's my cue," Charleston said, getting up from the table. "Come on, kids. Let's get some dessert."

Her children excitedly jumped from their seats and raced to the dessert table with Charleston laughing as she followed behind.

Edward rubbed his wife's back. "Settle down, Gail. Don't stoop to her level."

"I haven't begun to stoop yet. You know I'll put that woman out of my house."

Edward chuckled. "I know you will, but let's think of Jamie."

"Somebody needs to tell Jamie to run as fast as he can," Ms. Lucy chimed in, walking over and taking a seat at the table.

"Stop starting trouble, Lucille," Pastor Nelson lectured. "You can't tell a man who he should and shouldn't love. He'll only resent you for it."

Teylor thought about Pastor Nelson's words and silently debated whether it was the right time to profess her love for Jamie.

"I'm not starting anything, James. I've known that *man* since he was knee-high to a grasshopper, and Gail has been like my sister since I've been in this town. I love Jamie like he was my own son, and somebody needs to save him before he makes the biggest mistake of his life," Ms. Lucy countered.

"We've all known him since he was boy, and we all care about him, but that's a man, Lucille, and a man knows who he wants to be his wife."

Ms. Lucy turned her nose up in disgust. "Humph."

"Well, if that woman disrespects me or my child in my own home one more time, I'm putting her out. Jamie's feelings ain't gonna matter none at all if she does it again, you hear me?"

Edward continued to rub Gail's back as she took a deep breath to calm her nerves. He watched Jamie and Carrie on the dance floor. Then he spoke calmly, "Don't you worry about Jamie, Lucy. He'll do what's right. He always has."

Teylor looked at Jamie and Carrie, the duo brimming with laughter and love. Her heart sank a little lower, but she'd come too far to turn back now. Before the night was over, she would tell him her feelings, and she hoped with all of her might that Mr. Westbrook was right.

~

The evening eventually became less strained as the wine kept coming. After a couple hours, everyone seemed to be feeling weightless and genuinely enjoying themselves. They were dancing, delighting in the desserts, and chatting away.

Jamie was relieved. His future mother-in-law had managed to rub everyone the wrong way during dinner, including him. He hoped she'd warm up to him eventually, but it seemed a long shot. He watched his future in-laws cutting a rug on the dance floor alongside his parents, who were putting their own dent in the concrete. He smiled in admiration. His parents were everything he wanted himself and his wife to be.

Jamie stole a glance at Carrie, who sat at the dinner table talking with Charleston. A beautiful smile graced her lips. His niece and nephew ran up to Charlie to tell her something, briefly interrupting the conversation, before turning back and skipping into the house. Saber, Rima, and Teylor were gathered in a corner by the wine table, talking and laughing. Jamie watched Teylor for longer than he wanted to. She seemed to be listening more than talking. Something about her was different tonight. She was strikingly beautiful, in a way that he'd never seen her before, but something was still off about her. It was more than the hair and the dress. Although she looked gorgeous, he knew that it wasn't truly her.

What is she up to? He couldn't put his finger on it. He wondered if she could sense that he was going to tell her they could no longer be friends. A part of him wished she hadn't shown up so that he wouldn't have to go through with it. Then again, a part of him knew what he had to do if he wanted a successful marriage, even if it felt like it was going to kill him.

His eyes found their way back to his parents, and once again he smiled.

"You don't see that very often."

Ms. Lucy appeared by his side.

"What's that?" he asked.

Ms. Lucy inclined her head toward the Westbrooks. "Love like that. It's a rare thing."

Jamie slowly nodded in agreement. Keeping his eyes on his parents, he said, "Yeah. I hope to have that one day."

"You don't now?"

Jamie met her curious gaze. "I'm not saying that...I just..."

"It's not that hard to figure out, Jamie. Love like that is not unsure. You either have it or you don't."

Percy Sledge's *When a Man Loves a Woman* began to play, and Jamie watched as his parents snuggled close, staring into each other's eyes like they were seeing each other for the first time—adoration oozing from their smiles. He couldn't find the words to answer Ms. Lucy's question so he just watched in silence.

"Look at them," she continued. "I've known them for years, and I've watched them fall in love over and over and over and over again. The blessing they share is that they were sure, Jamie. They knew what they had, and they still know. So I ask you again," she said, turning back to him. "Is that what you have?"

Jamie was intimidated into silence. There was no way he could give her an answer because the truth was, he wasn't sure. He just stood there, hands in his pockets, battling within himself. Maybe, if it wasn't there now, it would come. Maybe a love like what his parents shared needed time to mature. Satisfying himself with that answer, he turned to Ms. Lucy and responded. "In time, Ms. Lucy. Everything with time."

Just then, Teylor approached them.

"Excuse me, Ms. Lucy, do you mind if I speak to Jamie for a moment?"

"Not at all, dear," she said as she turned to leave. She suddenly stopped and pivoted back to face Jamie.

"Or maybe, you just refuse to see it. Sometimes it's the most obvious things to which we are blind."

She locked eyes with Teylor and walked away with a knowing smile.

~

"Hey," Teylor said once they were alone.

Jamie's eyes traveled from her hair to her stilettos and back up to her eyes again.

"Well, look at you, Mahogany."

She gave a lopsided smile and slowly nodded her head. "Look at me," she echoed.

His eyes locked with hers, and the twinkle in his told her he approved, but when he kept his thoughts to himself, Teylor asked, "What?"

"Nothing, I just haven't seen you look like this in...I can't remember when."

She let off a sheepish laugh. "Is that a good thing?"

"You look beautiful, Teylor," he said plainly. "You should dress up more often. If you keep stepping out like this, you'll probably be getting married before I do," he added with a small chuckle.

Teylor stared at the ground. "Well, you're getting married next week so that's next to impossible."

The mood grew serious between them, and Teylor lifted her head to meet his gaze. Her stomach was doing somersaults, and she knew she had to act quickly before she lost her nerve.

"Do you wanna dance? We need to talk."

Jamie raised an eyebrow. "Do you want to dance or do you want to talk, Teylor?"

"Both."

Jamie frowned, but Teylor didn't care. She had to get this over with. "Jamie, please."

"Teylor, let's just walk through the garden and talk." His eyes traveled to Carrie, who was still chatting with Charleston. "I have some things I want to say to you too."

Her eyes pleaded with him as she held out her hand. "Dance with me."

Taking notice of the emotion in her eyes, Jamie stole another look at Carrie, who was now watching them, and then reluctantly relented.

As they were dancing, The Righteous Brothers' *Unchained Melody* began to play. They moved in silence for a moment, her arms around his shoulders, his around her waist. Teylor took slow easy breaths to calm herself before she changed her mind again. She raised her head to look at him. He glanced at their surroundings before he finally dropped his eyes to meet hers. He stared quietly at her for a moment.

Teylor held his stare, wanting him to read her heart without her having to say the words.

Finally, he spoke. "What did you want to talk about?"

Teylor opened her mouth, but nothing came out.

Just say it, she encouraged herself.

She saw Jamie raise his eyes and look past her. She turned her head to follow his gaze. Carrie stood just out of earshot, her eyes fixed on the two of them moving slowly with the music. Teylor knew that they were speaking a wordless language.

Carrie was silently calling Jamie to her.

His eyes pleaded for a few more minutes.

Time was running out.

Teylor nibbled on her bottom lip. Her heart felt like it would beat right out of her chest. Her legs threatened to give out, but she stood firm, building the boldness to go forward. She closed her eyes and became enveloped in the moment. Teylor then felt the lyrics to the song ushering her forward into the unknown. Being in his arms felt like where she belonged and where she wanted to remain.

"Teylor."

His voice was soft like warm butter, but held a melancholy note. He was getting ready to leave her.

Carrie was beckoning.

Teylor could feel her eyes burning a hole through her back.

The time was now.

He said her name again and this time, she looked up into his midnight eyes. Serious, dark, and focused on her own, she held his gaze and allowed her soul to reveal its hidden treasures.

"I'm in love with you, Jamie," she said barely above a whisper.

At her confession, Jamie froze.

His eyes became dazed, as if he'd just been dealt a harsh blow. Teylor swore he stopped breathing but she couldn't stop herself now. Their future depended on every word she could get out at this moment, and they sprung forth like rushing waters.

"That's it. What I've been trying to tell you, but couldn't. I've loved you since the eighth grade. You're the most special person I've ever known. I love how you love the Lord and your family, and how you're so caring to everyone around you. The way you play with your niece and nephew; how you always make me bless my food before I eat it."

Lines formed in his forehead, and his eyes were a mélange of emotions. Shock, fear, anger, and she could only hope...love.

Tears welled up in her own eyes and her voice quaked as she forced herself to finish what she'd started. "The way you caught me before I fainted when my mom died. How did you know to be there? You always know when to be there. You laid next to me and held me all night while I cried.

"I love the way you look at me." The tears came fully and rolled down her cheeks. "I love how you call me Mahogany. You make me feel so beautiful. You always have.

"I love how you're so protective of my heart. You're the love of my life, and there's no other man that I can imagine sharing my life with. That's why it's been killing me that you've chosen to live yours with someone else. I want to be your wife. I've always wanted to be your wife, Jamie. I'm hopelessly, undeniably in love with you."

"Hey, is it okay if I cut in?" Carrie stood next to them with a phony smile on her face that quickly faded when she saw the tears in Teylor's eyes and the shock in Jamie's.

"Is everything okay?"

Teylor halfway rolled her eyes. In her opinion, that question was being asked far too frequently lately. She wanted to shout to everyone that nothing was okay and everything was a mess, but instead, she wiped her tears, forced a smile, and walked away, leaving Carrie with lots of questions, and Jamie too stunned to answer them.

FOURTEEN

He must have replayed that dance a thousand times in his head, and he still couldn't make sense of what had happened.

Teylor is in love with me.

How could he not have known, or maybe he just hadn't wanted to see it.

Jamie sat in a chair at the dining table in his parents' backyard, his head hung low, shoulders slouched. He looked every bit of what he'd been through. The music had died down, the candles in the lanterns flickered as some were blown out by the night's breeze. Most of the guests had already gone, only Carrie and her parents lingered. Carrie had asked him repeatedly what was wrong after Teylor left, but he couldn't tell her. He'd simply walked away, retreating to his old bedroom. He'd eventually found his way back to the party after everyone had gone, thankful that he'd evaded their curious stares and questions. Now, Carrie was standing by the back door tossing fretful glances his way. He chose to ignore them. He also chose to ignore the disdainful stares coming from Debra King.

Another word out of her and he'd lose his cool, the little he had left, anyway.

His emotions were running wild, sending his heart on a wild goose chase. Jamie shut his eyes tight, hoping to get some clarity on what was now his life. He wasn't sure where he stood with his beautiful fiancée, and Teylor...Teylor was an entirely different situation altogether.

"Jamie."

Edward came toward him, hands in pockets, worry covering his face.

"Jamie, how are you, son?"

Jamie slowly shook his head, still keeping it low. His father placed his hand on Jamie's shoulder.

"Look, son, I'm going to take Carrie and her parents back to the hotel. I don't want you to have to worry about anything. Take all the time you need. Sleep in your old room tonight if you need to. I'll be back as soon as I can."

Edward walked away and led the Kings around the house to the front gate. Jamie could feel Carrie's eyes on him as she walked away. He let her go without so much as a glance.

Later that night, Jamie lay in the pitch dark of his old room, his forearm stretched across his forehead. There was no need to try to force sleep; it wouldn't be visiting him anytime soon. Images of Teylor wearing the body-hugging black dress, curls hanging down her back, saying *I'm in love with you, Jamie,* kept him stirred.

Why now?

One week before his wedding, she'd dropped an atomic-sized bomb on him.

A knock on the door disturbed his thoughts.

"Yeah," he called out.

"Jamie, it's Mom. Are you decent? Can I come in?"

Jamie sat up and swung his legs around to the side of the bed. He blindly reached the lamp switch and clicked it on.

"I'm decent, Mom."

Gail entered, her smile full of compassion. She'd changed into her lavender pajamas and leopard house slippers. The sight of his mother always instantly put him in a better mood, but tonight it was a challenge, even for her—still his lips curved into a smile.

"How was your evening, gorgeous?"

"Interesting, to say the least."

"Tell me about it," he agreed.

She sat beside him on the bed and rubbed his back.

"How's my boy?"

Jamie looked his mother in the eye and remained quiet. The sadness and despair in his stare answered her question.

"You wanna talk about it?" she asked.

He was silent for a long moment, and she waited. For her, patience was definitely a virtue.

"Teylor," he finally said in a quiet voice. "She told me she's in love with me."

Gail remained poker-faced. No shock showed in her features nor did any gasps escape from her lips. She was quiet.

Knowing.

Jamie couldn't help but let out a small chuckle. "You already knew, didn't you?"

She smiled.

He shook his head in disbelief.

"Why didn't she tell me sooner? Why now after all these years?"

"Fear, Jamie. She was scared of losing you."

"Teylor knows I would never hurt her."

"Not intentionally," Gail answered.

"Not ever," he corrected.

"Well, what do you think it did to her when she found out that you were engaged to Carrie?"

He didn't answer, but it all made sense. Things had been different between them ever since he'd broken the news to her. He was still having a hard time understanding why she'd waited so long though; she'd had ample time to tell him how she felt. Now they'd been friends for too long. Things might have been different. He loved Teylor more than he loved himself and would have done anything to make her happy, including love her in the way she wanted him to, but now...now it was too late. He was getting married. He loved Carrie and the thought of breaking her heart tore at him. He'd always been the protector, the mender. Hurting either of them would make him a destroyer, and they would all have to live with whatever decision he made.

Jamie tried to fight them but the tears were persistent. His eyes began to water, and he dropped his head.

"I would have loved her the way she needed me to, if she would have said something sooner."

"I know you would have, but what would that have profited either of you? If the only way you could love her romantically was out of a sense of obligation, a wish to make her happy? That's not the kind of love she needs from you—or wants. You must love her in that way because you want to, not because you feel like you should, or she asked you to. She deserves more than that, Jamie...and so do you."

"But love is a choice. I would have chosen to love her as my wife. You know that."

"I know, son."

"What am I supposed to do now, Mom?"

Gail embraced him. He hated for her to see him this way. He knew it pained her to watch him in such agony, mainly because it happened so rarely, but his heart was so tender when it came to the women in his life, and she knew he was falling apart.

"Well, I can tell you this. First, you need to figure out where your heart is. Don't make a hasty decision in the beginning; you could do a lot more damage later on that way. Your love should be genuine, Jamie, not forced. Don't force yourself to be with either woman if your heart's not there. As far as who to choose, I can't tell you that, son. This is your life. You have to make that decision because you're the one who has to live with it."

"I'm not sure that I can live with hurting either of them," he said, his voice weaker than before.

She turned his head toward her and met his tear-filled gaze.

"You can and you will. Think about this, Jamie. If you believe that it would have been so easy for you to fall in love with Teylor just to make her happy, do you think that maybe you already are?"

Jamie let her question hang.

"You know where to find the answer, Jamie." Her tone was stern but loving. She kissed him on the forehead and walked toward the door. Before leaving, she turned to him and said, "Do what you do best, son," and walked out, closing the door behind her.

Knowing what she meant, Jamie got down on his knees. Too wounded to speak, he allowed the waterfall of tears to pour down his face and do the praying for him.

~

The next morning, Jamie was up with the sun. He left his parents' house and drove home. He was still unsure of his feelings, but after praying off and on all night, his weight was a little lighter. Answers would come; he was sure of it.

When Jamie exited the elevator, Carrie was sitting outside of his door, forcing him to stop in his tracks. Her bloodshot eyes met his, and his heart sank. He knew that they would have to talk eventually, but he wasn't ready to face her. He needed more time to gather his thoughts.

"Hey," she said quietly, standing.

"Carrie. Hey."

He'd never seen her this way before. Her eyes were puffy, bags settled underneath. Her hair was tied in a haphazard ponytail, and she wore white jogging pants and a coral tank top. By the looks of her, she too had had a sleepless night.

"How long have you been waiting out here?" he asked.

She shrugged. "An hour, maybe."

Awkward silence filled the air as they studied each other.

Finally she said, "I couldn't sleep."

He nodded in agreement. "Neither could I—I stayed at my parents' last night."

It was breaking his heart to know that he was the reason for her anguish, and the thought of what Teylor might be experiencing was too much to bear. Jamie wrapped his arm around Carrie and opened the door to his apartment.

"Can I make you some breakfast? Do you want anything to drink?"

Carried sat down on the sectional sofa.

"No, thanks. I don't really have an appetite."

Jamie sat next to her and looked into her eyes. When they began to water, he wiped an escaped tear from her cheek. Carrie looked down at her hands, avoiding eye contact with him, and he knew it was coming.

"What happened last night, Jamie?"

Jamie looked away immediately. He wasn't sure what to tell her. He always stood on the truth, but seeing the pain in her eyes made the truth an enemy. He forced himself to face her again. Hurtful or not, she deserved the truth and nothing less.

"Carrie...I—"

"She told you, didn't she?"

Jamie went still.

"Told me what?" he asked hesitantly.

Carrie's voice was gentle but confident. "That she's in love with you."

Jamie's eyes grew wide. "How—"

"I confronted her," she said, cutting him off. "At Lucy's. Three days ago." She shook her head, recalling the incident. "She never admitted it, but she never denied it."

Jamie was stunned into silence. Carrie had never mentioned her and Teylor's encounter, but everything was all starting to come together. She was so adamant about him ending his friendship with Teylor because she'd already known how Teylor felt about him.

"I saw it in her eyes, Jamie. And when I told her that we'd moved the wedding date to next week, she became sick."

"What do you mean?" he asked.

"She ran into the restaurant's bathroom and puked. That's what I mean."

Jamie briefly closed his eyes. How had he managed to hurt two women that meant so much to him? The vision of Teylor being physically sick made him nauseous. He'd known she was hurting but he had no idea how bad it was. He clenched his jaw and breathed deeply, calming his insides. When he looked at Carrie again, she was crying. He remained quiet, knowing that he couldn't find the right words to comfort her. He could tell her that he was sure she was the one for him and she had nothing to worry about when it came to Teylor, but he'd be lying.

"Look at you, Jamie. Even now, worry and concern for her is written all over your face. It's killing you knowing that you've hurt her, isn't it?"

"It's killing me knowing that I've hurt you, Carrie," he said.

He attempted to take her hands in his but she quickly snatched them away.

"It should. I'm going to be your wife," she said sternly. "But what about her, Jamie? Are you in love with her?"

This was the second time he'd been asked that question about Teylor, and he responded the way he had the first time—with silence. In the past, he probably would have laughed if asked, but now, he was forced to ponder the answer for his future happiness depended upon it. If the answer was no, then why was it so hard to let Teylor go? Why did the possibility of living life without her remind him of a world without the sun? Why was he so sure that he would have made her his wife had Teylor told him about her feelings before he'd met Carrie? He thought back to Saber's question the night of the gathering. *Ten years on an island.*

As if reading his mind, Carrie said, "Ten years...on the island, Jamie. Who's it going to be? Your mouth said me, but somehow I feel like your heart was saying something different."

She rose from the couch.

"I love you, Jamie, and I'm willing to fight for you, but you have to decide what and who you want. You can't have us both. I'll give you some time to think about it, but I won't wait around forever."

FIFTEEN

The entire next day, Teylor was a ball of nerves. Having to see Jamie—and probably Carrie—tonight at Rima's café was taking a toll on her nervous system. She barely got any sleep last night, and eating was near impossible.

Jamie hadn't called or stopped by so she had no clue how he was taking her confession, but she couldn't miss Rima's show. Teylor paced most of the day, forcing herself to attempt writing, but to no avail. Reading was also a no-go, and she absolutely refused to venture into town for fear of running into Jamie, or even worse, Carrie. She briefly contemplated the idea of not attending Rima's showcase but quickly thought better of it as she just couldn't afford to lose any more friends.

The day shuffled on a lot faster than Teylor would have liked and before she knew it, she was searching her closet for an outfit to suit the occasion. Realizing last night's attire might have been a bit out of character, she opted for something more her usual style— skinny jeans, a loose gold tank, and matching strappy heels. The hair she liked, so she kept her curls loose. Her infamous red pout and gold hoops finished her look, and Teylor was satisfied. She'd be comfortably herself tonight, even if the evening brought an awkward air. Regardless of what was to come, Teylor wouldn't back down. She was tired of running, tired of hiding her true feelings.

Maybe she was being selfish, but what choice did she have? Letting Jamie marry Carrie without him knowing how she truly felt would be a crime against her own heart. She had to at least give him a chance to love her back—the same way she loved him. If he still chose Carrie, she was simply going to have to move on. Above anything, his happiness was most important to her and if Carrie did the job, then so be it.

One last glimpse in the mirror, a prayer for good measure, and Teylor was out the door.

~

Songbird Café was lively. Throngs of people occupied the space, drinking caffeinated beverages and eating a variety of foods from the special menu created by Connie for the evening. A small stage housing a pianist, drummer, and standing microphone had been set up on the far right of the café. Tables and chairs filled the rest of the space, and a giant disco ball hung above the stage, creating colorful lights that bounced off the walls. The lighting was dim, and the crowd patiently awaited their performer.

Jamie entered the café and walked over to the table positioned directly in front of the stage, reserved for him and their small circle of friends. Charlie was already seated and surprisingly, Jonathan was next to her. Jamie saw Saber working the room, smiling and charming as many single women as he could. He laughed, shaking his head, and went to greet his sister and brother-in-law.

"Hey, lil brother," Charlie exclaimed when she saw Jamie. Jamie kissed her on the cheek and gave Jonathan a firm handshake.

"Man, I thought you were missing," he joked to his brother-in-law.

Jonathan let out a hardy laugh and said, "Nah, man. Been working a lot. You know how it is."

Jamie nodded and added, "Well, we miss you around here. Don't be a stranger."

He locked eyes with Charlie, who gave him a small eye roll. He wondered if she'd ever asked Jonathan about him having an affair and made a mental note to quiz her later. She looked happier tonight, so he was hoping that was a sign that things had turned around for the better.

Jamie took a seat next to Charlie at the end of the table and noticed three other empty seats. One for Saber, and he figured the other two were for Teylor and Carrie.

He'd rather have skipped the event altogether if it meant not having to come face-to-face with those two, but he reminded himself that tonight was about Rima.

His sister leaned over and whispered, "I've been meaning to ask you what happened last night."

"Don't," he whispered back.

Charlie apparently heard the seriousness in his voice because she let it go. Jamie sucked in a deep breath and forced himself to gain control. A quick glance toward the entryway made his stomach twist in knots. Standing by the door, casually dressed yet stunningly beautiful was Teylor. Her eyes connected with his, and it brought emotions he'd never felt before. He saw her chest rise and fall and knew her nerves were just as frazzled as his own. She walked toward their table, and he braced himself.

Here goes nothing.

~

The dim café gave Teylor jazz club vibes. Even though it was filled with people, the mood was mellow. Teylor waved and said hellos to a few of the people she knew. Locking eyes with Jamie when she'd first walked in had almost made her want to turn the other way and head back home, but she was determined to face her fears. And she would support Rima. A quick inhale and exhale relaxed her a bit, and she decided she was up for the challenge.

As she made her way to their reserved table, a confidence she didn't recognize invaded her. She reached the table and said hello. Charlie and Jonathan stood to greet her with hugs and smiles. She was surprised to see Jonathan but elated to see that the couple had reunited. Jonathan had missed so many events in the past month, she'd started to worry that there might be marriage trouble. Seeing him tonight relieved her fears.

Teylor always thought they made an attractive couple. Jonathan was extremely handsome with vanilla wafer skin, dark wavy hair, and sepia eyes. His faded beard and thick mustache were always clean and neatly trimmed. These two had been some of the most gorgeous teenagers in town, and Teylor had thought they were a match made in heaven when they'd finally started going out.

Then Jamie stood from his chair, and instead of waiting for him to come to her, she walked over to him. Their eyes held briefly before she said, "Hey, Jamie, how are you?"

Not giving him time to answer, she wrapped her arms around his neck and embraced him. She felt him stiffen for a moment and then relax. She didn't take it personally. She realized how awkward things must be for him. They were for her too, but only because she no longer saw him as a friend. He was now the man she was in love with.

"I'm good, Teylor. How are you?"

When they parted, she answered him honestly. "I've been better."

He looked away. "Yeah, me too."

"Is it that hard for you to look at me now, Jamie?" she asked with a small chuckle.

His gaze returned to her. "Not hard, just different."

"Well, things are different now."

Their gazes lingered in silence. Those beautiful eyes of his were staring at her as if he was trying to figure out who she now was. She didn't mind. Teylor wanted him to see her differently. Up until last night, he'd always looked at her as his best friend, now it was time for him to see her as more than that. Much more.

He opened his mouth to speak when Saber walked up and seized their moment.

"T!" he shouted, hugging her. "Glad you made it."

"Of course I made it. Why wouldn't I?"

He exchanged an awkward glance with Jamie.

Charlie and Jonathan watched as if they were at a live taping of a soap opera.

"No reason," he said. "I'm just glad you're here."

To Jamie, he asked, "Is Carrie coming?"

Jamie eyed the door and shrugged. "I couldn't tell ya, man."

Saber nodded his understanding and took a seat next to Teylor.

The spotlight highlighted the microphone, and Rima graced the stage wearing a white, floor-length bohemian dress with puffy sleeves that hung loosely off her shoulders. She let her crimson locks flow freely and a white and pink hibiscus flower rested above her right ear.

"How y'all doing tonight?" she asked in a low melodic tone.

The crowd answered with claps and some even shouted, "Alright now."

"I appreciate you all being in the house tonight. You could've been anywhere in the world, but you're here with me," she said with a wink.

A few more shouts came from the audience.

"If you don't mind, I'd like to get the night started with Ms. Anita Baker. Is that alright with y'all?"

"YEAH!"

The drummer and pianist started playing Baker's *Sweet Love*, and the crowd moved with the tune. Rima rocked and swayed her dress and when she approached the mic, her voice lit up the room.

Teylor sang along with Rima and threw her hands in the air. Every word Rima uttered, Teylor felt.

She allowed herself to be caught up in the moment, tuning out everyone that surrounded her. How could Ms. Baker so perfectly express Teylor's life? She almost forgot where she was until the applause broke her out of her trance. Teylor joined in, glancing around to see if anyone had noticed her reverie, only to find Jamie staring back at her. He looked away before she did.

"Thank you. Thank you so much," Rima cooed, then belted out a couple more R&B classics.

Teylor was enjoying herself, despite her troubles. During a brief intermission, Teylor went to the counter to order an iced chai. It was a slight variation from her normal hot chai, but she was feeling change in the air and to her surprise, welcomed it. Somehow she believed it could be a change for the better, especially where it concerned her and Jamie; but as quick as those optimistic views entered her mind, they were gone just as fast when she glanced toward the entrance.

There Carrie stood, a superior beauty, stunning in a body-hugging, white lace mini-dress and gold open-toed high heels. A dark mane of large barrel curls cascaded down her back, and she gave it a flip when she noticed all eyes on her.

Teylor's heart dropped to her stomach at the sight of Carrie. Everything suddenly began to go in slow motion. Teylor's eyes traveled to Jamie and what she saw pained her. He was mesmerized by Carrie, and who could blame him? The entire room seemed to be taken by her arrival. Teylor knew she could never compete with that. What confidence she had found quickly exited, and she wanted to do the same. She looked at Carrie again, and this time her eyes were expectant. Teylor saw the faintest smile cover her lips, and with another hair flip, Carrie sashayed toward their table with Jamie's eyes glued to her.

When she reached the group, Jamie stood and greeted her with a tight hug and a kiss on the cheek. Teylor knew it was over. The hope she had of her and Jamie being more than friends evaporated. The look in his eyes, the way he embraced her; he was in love with Carrie and there was nothing more Teylor could do about it. She had to accept it and try her best to move on with her own life.

Jaimie moved seats to be next to Carrie. He hadn't done that for Teylor. He didn't even turn around to see if she was okay, like he would normally have done. She slowly lowered her head and prayed for strength.

The lights dimmed, signaling that intermission was over and the show was resuming. Rima was back on the mic, and as much as Teylor wanted to continue to support her friend, she'd had all she could take. She wouldn't stay around and be belittled by Jamie and Carrie any longer.

Not tonight.

She was breaking.

The room grew silent. All Teylor could hear was the sound of her racing heart. She took slow steady breaths to keep herself sane and decided it was time to leave. She lifted her head to see Jamie looking in her direction. He'd finally noticed her.

No.

Charlie, Jonathan, and Saber were all looking at her. Teylor tried focusing on what was happening, and suddenly she heard her name being called.

"Teylor."

It was Rima onstage saying her name.

"Are you ready?" she asked.

Teylor was confused until she remembered that Rima had asked her to recite a poem during her set. She'd been enthused at the time because she already had a piece in mind. Now, Teylor wanted to disappear. She wanted to shake her head and tell her friend she wasn't feeling well and had to leave, but all eyes were now on her. She had to woman up and do what she'd promised.

Teylor's legs felt like jelly as she made her way to the stage. She wasn't sure how she was going to get through this, but she had to at least try. She grabbed the mic with one hand and looked out into the audience, refusing to even glance at the table that housed her friends. The slightest bit of eye contact with Jamie and she would bolt. Teylor took a deep breath and cleared her throat, ignoring the waves tossing in her stomach.

"Ummm…when Rima asked me to do this, at first I was excited," she started in a shaky voice. "But now…" Her voice trailed off.

She glanced at Rima who gave her a reassuring look. Teylor offered a small nod and decided to take a different direction. She was unsure about a lot of things in life, but one thing was certain—she could write.

"You know sometimes, life deals you situations that leave you feeling lost...or empty."

A few people from the crowd shouted out their agreement by saying "Preach" and "Come on now."

"Especially when it comes to loving someone," Teylor continued.

"Amen," an observer yelled.

"Sometimes you can love someone so deeply and..." Teylor's eyes finally landed on Jamie's. They held on, communicating without speaking. This time, Teylor didn't know what his eyes were saying. She didn't know anything anymore. Seeing him there, next to Carrie, sparked something in her—more courage perhaps. She was tired. Tired of guessing how he felt about her, tired of crying, of feeling helpless. Tired of fighting for him to love her.

She was tired of it all.

Teylor stood tall and put back her shoulders. She looked straight into the crowd and said, "But what happens when that person doesn't love you back? When you've given this person all of you, down to your identity? What happens when the only person you have left to love is yourself?"

She saw a few heads nod in the audience.

"I wrote this poem for someone special, but like they so often do, things changed...so I'll start with that and go wherever my thoughts lead me. There is no title, but I hope you guys feel my heart. Here goes."

Another deep breath escaped from Teylor and she began.

"Loving you was easy...it always has been,

And I'll offer it eternally, as long as I never see its end.

You can't imagine how many times I've dreamt of what it would be like to taste your kiss.

I know it's reminiscent of honey, agave's nectar, the darkest chocolate, take your pick.

Mmmm, speaking of chocolate brings me to the expression of your skin, darkened by the sun's pucker, resembling powerful kings from Mother Africa's den."

Teylor started to freestyle the next lines of her poem, not giving any thought to what she might say. She allowed the words to take over, and what was inside of her to pour out.

"Yes, it's true…the love I have for you can be compared to no other, yet I must sit in agony and watch you love another. I smile but it's killing me and I have the choice to break and surrender to the pain…but my heavenly Father has assured me that I have too much to gain…to walk around defeated and dejected.

"So, dear Heartbreak, if it's me you're looking for, I must reject you. I'm done asking for love when love is the reason that I'm here. And with it I know that I can cast out every fear."

Teylor's eyes began to water, and she closed them and let the tears fall. She no longer felt ashamed of her pain. With every word, she felt chains breaking and falling off of her. She was liberating herself.

"So, Tears, come if you must—rinse me clean with each one that I cry. I'm done looking for what's already inside. And because I've been set free, I no longer have to hide. Dear Pain, this is not an ode to self-empowerment, this is me saying…goodbye."

Teylor slowly opened her eyes to a standing ovation. Whistles and shouts of approval were hailing from the audience. Teylor was blown away by the response. She swallowed the lump in her throat. Even though she was already crying, she was on the verge of breaking out into sobs. Not from sadness, but because she felt free. She'd given herself away fully on that stage, not caring what anyone would think. She'd needed to do it for herself. And she had. Seeing the crowd's reaction was just a bonus. She didn't look at Jamie. She didn't need to. It wasn't about him anymore.

She was letting him go.

Teylor nodded her head at the audience—her silent thank-you. She gazed at Rima, who had tears in her eyes and a smile on her face. She didn't have to say anything; Teylor knew her friend was proud. She glanced at the audience again and was proud of herself. Having done what she'd unknowingly come to do, Teylor walked off the stage and right out of the door.

SIXTEEN

The next morning Teylor sat at the lake's edge wrapped in a blanket. She'd gotten no sleep again, and her thoughts were still pondering the previous night's events. Usually, sleepless nights meant she'd lain awake trying to bear the agony she'd been feeling, but not this time. There was no anguish, no despair, and no sadness. She'd simply been too excited to sleep.

After pouring her heart out onstage, she'd gone home and written three chapters in her book. She felt more inspired than she had in a long time—like she could conquer the world. She'd even decided to forgo church this morning. She needed the time to herself to regroup.

Teylor felt at peace as she watched the wind make ripples in the water. The temperature was about seventy degrees, and the air was crisp. The forecast called for rain, and she was ready for it. Any other time when it rained, Teylor's mood would match the sky. The lack of sunshine often left her down and out, even though her mother used to say that rain meant that God was cleansing something or someone.

Today Teylor agreed. He was cleansing her and she would welcome it.

Just as her heart was saying "thank you," the sky let out a soft rumble. She smiled because she knew He'd heard her. Lately, all she'd been doing was communing with God—more than she had in her entire life, or at least it felt that way. She remembered Jamie telling her that God would sometimes use the pain caused from their own mistakes to bring His children closer to Him. In this case, it was true. When her mother had died, Teylor hadn't prayed as much as she'd been doing since Jamie told her he'd asked Carrie to marry him. In a way she was thankful for that. Before then, Teylor couldn't remember the last time she'd spoken to Him.

She raised her eyes and looked at the ash colored sky with its dreary appearance, inhaling the scent of the rain that would soon make an appearance. She always loved the smell. In the book of Psalms, the sixty-fifth chapter and ninth verse, the Bible says that God visits the earth and waters it. Teylor now hoped in that verse. She needed God to visit her and rain his rich mercy and blessing in her life. She knew that she would overcome losing her best friend, but the pain still lingered. She refused to be taken by the loss, but she'd be delusional to think that she didn't need help from a more powerful source.

Like she'd said in her poem, she loved him so much that somehow, without realizing it, he'd become her identity. Everything was centered on him. That was her mistake. No one or nothing should have ever taken the place of God in her life, but that's who Jamie was in hers. As amazing as he was, he was not, nor would he ever be, God, even though he was a major reason for her seeking Him.

Jamie loved the Lord and often encouraged her through Scriptures and prayers to develop her own relationship with Him. Not that she hadn't wanted to, but Teylor was unsure if she ever had before he came along. Her mother never taught her anything about the Bible, or any religion for that matter. She'd mention His name in passing, but there were no family Bible studies like Jamie and his family held every week. The only time her mother ever went to church was on special holidays, like Easter and Christmas, but she'd never deterred Teylor from going with Jamie and his family every Sunday. Teylor figured that maybe she thought Teylor would find whatever she had been looking for. Peace.

Now, looking up toward the heavens, Teylor had hope. Hope that her mother had found the peace that she was initially looking for in all the wrong places, but most of all, hope that she herself would find it fully before she left this earth. Teylor took a deep breath as a reassuring calmness swept over her. She reminded herself of the verse she'd just read the other day in the Book of John, chapter fourteen and verse twenty-seven:

Peace I leave with you, My peace I give to you. I do not give to you as the world gives. Do not let your hearts be troubled and do not be afraid.

Taking in the rain-scented air, Teylor looked up to the sky once more. She couldn't see Him, but she most definitely felt Him. With more faith than she'd ever had before, she believed that He was with her and would hear her, so she spoke.

"Heavenly Father, I'm so sorry. Sorry that it's taken me this long to realize how much I need you. Honestly, I'm not sure I ever really believed you were real. I only went along with what Jamie told me. Now I'm sitting here and I can feel you with me, more than I ever have. Why couldn't I before?"

Tears stung her eyes.

"I think of everything I've been through and how Jamie was always there. I guess I always figured it was him and not You, but I once heard the pastor say that You love us through people. Now I know that it was You. It's always been You, loving me through Jamie. The love I so desperately wanted from him, I was really needing from You. Forgive me for giving another Your glory, Lord. You're all I need. You're all I'll ever need. I'm so unsure of many things still, but this I know for certain; You will never leave nor forsake me. I thank you, Father, and I give You all the praise and honor."

She allowed her tears to fall and as if on cue, the rain fell from the clouds.

The washing had begun.

~

Jamie and Carrie were driving back to Spirit Lake from Phoenix. He had some work to catch up on in the office and had asked Carrie to come along. Her parents decided to catch up on some rest back at the hotel, which gave Carrie a little free time, and he was happy when she agreed. He was ready to make things right between them. They'd spent most of the morning together, having breakfast in the city; she'd done some shopping while he'd gone to the office. Jamie had even skipped church, which was rare for him, but he'd needed a moment to forget the troubles that surrounded him in Spirit Lake. Before heading back, they grabbed lunch at True Food Kitchen.

"We'll definitely have to eat here more often after we're married, Jamie."

He nodded in agreement. "I figured you'd like it."

She smiled.

He was relieved that Teylor hadn't come up in conversation, but he wasn't sure if Carrie was purposely avoiding the topic or waiting for the right time to spring it on him. He hoped for the former. Things were going well, and he wanted to keep it that way. He found relief in the fact that she no longer seemed upset with him. After Teylor's stunt last night at the café, he knew Carrie would be up in arms, but she'd never even mentioned it. Maybe she hadn't given it a second thought. He, on the other hand, couldn't stop thinking about it.

The way Teylor had described wanting to kiss him, how much she loved him. For a moment, it had felt like it was just the two of them in the room, but the part that really plagued him was the last line.

This is me saying…goodbye.

What did she mean by that?

Was it really happening?

Was she really letting him go?

Carrie was special to him, and Jamie still planned on marrying her, yet the thought of a final goodbye to Teylor was more difficult than he'd imagined, and was part of the reason for his delay in telling her that their friendship was over. He still couldn't come to terms with that thought, even though he knew it was necessary. Then, there stilled lingered the unanswered question: Was he in love with Teylor? Jamie shook his head at nothing in particular.

"Is that a no?"

Carrie's voice snapped him out of his thoughts. He hadn't heard a word she'd been saying.

"I'm sorry, sweetheart. What was that?"

Carrie's voice was concerned when she asked, "What are you thinking about?"

Her brows drew together, and he knew he had to quiet her worries or things would take a turn for the worst. He hated to lie, but he didn't have the energy to quarrel.

"Sorry, sweetheart. We had some issues at work. Some loads didn't get covered, and I was just trying to think of a solution."

Not exactly a lie. There had been a few uncovered loads, though he'd solved that problem before he left the office, but if he could prevent a future problem by not telling Carrie he'd been thinking about Teylor, then he wouldn't. She seemed satisfied with his answer.

"I was asking you if we could go to the lake today. Maybe take my parents?"

Jamie stopped chewing his food.

"We haven't been since I've been in town."

There is a reason for that.

She waited for an answer. Jamie continued to chew his food slowly. He hadn't taken Carrie to the lake because that's where Teylor lived. More preventative measures.

Carrie eyed him. "Is there some reason you don't want me to go to the lake?"

He looked at her but didn't say anything. His eyes did the speaking for him.

"Ah," she said, nodding. "The infamous Teylor strikes again."

Great. Just what he'd been trying to avoid. This time he would be honest with her.

"I'm only trying to keep the peace between everyone," he said calmly.

"And how are you doing that exactly?"

Jamie took a sip of honey lemonade.

"Is it a crime to go to the lake just because she lives near it? What are you afraid of, Jamie? That she'll see us, two people who are to be wed in less than a week, together?"

"I don't want her to think I'm throwing it in her face."

Carrie threw her napkin on the table and shook her head. She let out a small chuckle.

"You never cease to amaze me, Jameson. I'm the one whose feelings should be of more concern to you," she said, pointing at her chest. "How do you think this makes me feel?"

"Your feelings concern me a great deal, Carrie."

"But not more than hers?"

"I didn't say that."

"You didn't have to. You've been showing me since I arrived."

She folded her arms across her chest and looked away from him. Jamie felt helpless. There was no way he could win in this dilemma. Whenever he tried to consider Teylor, he ended up hurting Carrie and vice versa. Why did he even bother?

He looked at Carrie, the stunning beauty who would soon be his wife. She wore her jet-black hair bone straight with a middle part, diamond studs glistened in her lobes, and she exuded elegance in a white floor-length maxi dress. Any man would be considered blessed to have her as his wife—why was he making it so difficult?

Last night, Saber had told him that marrying Carrie was the easy way out because then he didn't have to address how he really felt about Teylor. He'd brushed him off at the time, but now he thought about his words.

He recalled the reasons Teylor said she loved him. Everything she'd mentioned was who he really was, the core of him. He loved the Lord and his family. He genuinely cared about everyone around him, including her. Especially her. She'd said that he made her feel beautiful when he called her Mahogany, and she was. Everything about her was beautiful. But she was his best friend and Carrie was his fiancée.

He continued staring at the woman he would wed in a few days, wondering what her answers would be.

"Carrie, what do you love about me?"

Carrie threw an irritated glance his way. "Excuse me?"

He knew she was annoyed but he wasn't backing down. She'd never told him what she loved about him and here they were, less than a week away from their wedding.

"What do you love about me?" he repeated, his voice sterner this time.

"Really, Jamie? Timing is not your strong suit, is it?"

He stared her in the eye without blinking. He wanted her to know how serious he was. "Answer the question, Carrie."

She paused for a moment and took a deep breath. "I love everything about you, Jamie."

"Could you be more specific?"

She shrugged. "You're brilliant, successful, loving, handsome...would you like me to go on?"

He shook his head and took another bite of food.

"Where is this all coming from?" she asked.

Jamie met her eyes. "I just wanted to know."

On the ride back home they were silent. Jamie thought about Carrie's response to his question—generalized answers. He wasn't sure if that was his fault or not. Maybe he hadn't showed her the love she needed from him. Maybe he'd been too worried about Teylor to give himself fully to her. Of course Teylor knew him better. They'd been in each other's lives since they were thirteen. They'd spent more time together than they had with anyone else.

Suddenly he understood why Carrie was so upset. Teylor was getting the most of him, not his future wife. He would have to make some tough decisions. If Teylor was ready to say goodbye, then he'd be ready also. Like she said last night, things change and he had to move on. He grabbed Carrie's hand.

"Let's go to the lake when we get back to town."

She agreed with a smile, and Jamie was already starting to feel better about where his new life was heading.

SEVENTEEN

By early afternoon, the rain had given way to sun and the clouds had moved on, leaving the day warm and the lake crowded. It seemed like everyone in town was trying to beat the humidity that the showers left behind. Jamie and Carrie searched for an open space to set up their chairs and umbrellas but that proved to be a difficult task. Jamie's shoulders dropped when he saw that the only spot available had a perfect view of Teylor's cottage.

"Is there something wrong with this spot, honey?" Carrie asked when she saw Jamie's countenance fall.

He forced a smile and shook his head. They set up shop and spoke to their neighbors. Practically everyone knew each other, which was what made coming to the lake a special event.

"Maybe we can take the boat out in a few," Carrie suggested.

Jamie agreed.

He was still somewhat nervous about running into Teylor, but he concentrated on pushing those feelings aside. Today would be about him and Carrie. It was never his intention to hurt Teylor, and he hoped she'd understand, after all, she knew his heart.

But even more than the fear of running into Teylor, what ran through his mind most were the memories. He and Teylor had spent countless days and hours at the lake over the years. His eyes wandered to the spot where she'd almost drowned when they were in eighth grade. It had scared him so much that after jumping in to save her, he'd forced her to let him teach her to swim, threatening to never come back to the lake with her if she wouldn't learn. She'd obliged and Jamie had spent two months teaching her how to float and at least swim to safety. Before long, Teylor looked as though she'd been swimming her entire life. From that moment on, they barbequed, took the boat out, and had parties whenever they could.

He remembered her constantly looking across the lake at the cottages, asserting that she'd one day live in the high country. At the time, he'd told her he didn't understand why she'd want to live outside of town and that he'd never come and visit her way out there. He'd been wrong. He'd been there every chance he got. He was willing to do anything for her, and now, with regret gnawing at his gut, he realized that all of that would soon be over.

"Jamie."

Jamie snapped out of his musing and faced Carrie.

"That's been happening a lot lately."

"What?"

"You're daydreaming. Again. You haven't heard a word I've said," she accused.

Once again feeling a tinge of regret, he forced a soft smile. Here he was with his fiancée and all he could do was think of Teylor. How long would that continue to happen? Would Teylor's face fill his thoughts during the most intimate times with his wife? Would their memories overshadow the ones he intended to make with Carrie? He should hope not, but then again, his brain wasn't exactly cooperating.

Jamie placed a light kiss on Carrie's lips. Skepticism lingered in her eyes but she welcomed the affection.

"I'm sorry, beautiful. What did you say?"

"I asked if you were ready to take the boat out."

"Yeah, come on."

Jamie took her hand and led her to where the boats were docked.

~

Teylor could hear the good time everyone was having on the lake from inside of her writing room. After writing two chapters and beginning the next enough to avoid an annoying case of writer's block, she decided she was done for the day. She changed into her fuchsia one-piece bathing suit with its black sheer cover, and went to join the fun.

As soon as she stepped outside, the humidity hit her like a ton of bricks. She walked toward the dock at the foot of her backyard to take a seat and watch all the activity. Beads of sweat were already forming on her hairline and nose. She wiped them away and fanned herself with her hand.

Lucy's granddaughter, Sandy, came blowing by in a boat driven by a male that Teylor had never seen before. He was definitely from out of town. Sandy waved excitedly with a huge grin on her face as they passed by. Teylor waved back, laughing. She took her flip-flops off and submerged her feet in the water. She sloshed them back and forth as she glanced across the lake. Since most of the business in town closed on Sundays, she guessed half of the community was there.

Teylor heard another boat coming toward her and froze when she recognized the occupants.

Jamie and Carrie.

His back was to her and Teylor went unnoticed until Carrie, cheesing from ear to ear caught her eye. Her grin faded into a wicked smile when she noticed Teylor. Teylor looked away and tried to focus on the other happenings at the lake. Carrie had been so nice when they'd first met; now she could hardly stand the sight of Teylor, not that she could blame her. If she were in Carrie's shoes, she'd be just as angry; but Carrie had nothing to worry about. Teylor was done pursuing Jamie.

Another boat came toward her but slowed as it approached. When Teylor saw that it was Rima, she let out a sigh of relief. Rima docked her boat and joined Teylor on the pier.

"Hey there, Ms. Maya Angelou," she said cheerfully.

Teylor blushed. "Hey, sunshine."

Rima did emulate sunshine in her yellow, retro high-waist bikini and matching floppy straw hat. She plopped down next to Teylor and took her hat off.

"My God, it's hot out here!" she shouted.

Teylor nodded her agreement.

"You plan on jumping in?" Rima asked.

With a shrug, Teylor answered, "I thought about it. Still deciding."

"Well, you can at least take a boat ride with me."

"Maybe in a few. How long do you plan on hanging out?"

"Girl, who knows."

Rima looked out at the lake and spotted Jamie and Carrie getting out of his boat.

"I'm proud of you," she finally said.

Teylor grinned and said, "I'm proud of myself."

"As well as you should be."

Their eyes followed Jamie and Carrie to their chairs, positioned directly across from them. "If you could have seen his face," Rima said with a pleased smile.

"I didn't care to see it," Teylor admitted. "I was tired of caring."

"Well, at least you did it. You can live with the fact that you now know."

"Very true. I'm glad I did it." Teylor paused before adding, "I'm not quite sure where I go from here though."

"You go on. Just go on living. Life is still worth that…with or without him."

Teylor let out a long sigh. "I know."

"So what came over you last night?" Rima asked, turning to face her. "I know I asked you to recite something but I had no idea…"

Taylor slowly shook her head and thought back to what she'd been feeling onstage. "I'm not sure, Rima. It's like this power surge just traveled through me...this sense of confidence and courage I've never felt before. Seeing the two of them there together was about to rip me apart, but it was like, from the despair came something else. Something better. I can't explain it."

"Sounds like you just did."

Rima smiled and wrapped an arm around Taylor hugging her. Taylor returned the gesture.

"Like I said, I'm proud of you, girl."

~

Jamie was relieved the day at the lake had been uneventful and drama free. For a moment, he thought he'd lose his cool when he saw Taylor sitting on her dock, but he managed to pull it together; even going as far as to reposition himself in the boat so that he wouldn't be faced with her when he sped by. He also forced himself to be absorbed in conversation with Carrie so he wouldn't attempt a look at her as they'd sat across from her cottage. All in all, he and Carrie had had a good time, and he was still thanking God for that mercy. Now, he was back home getting ready to have dinner with Carrie and her parents. The Kings had opted out of going to the lake earlier, which also helped to alleviate some of Jamie's stress. He was praying that God would give him a double dose of mercy and things would go smoothly, because his last encounter with Mrs. King was not one he wanted to relive.

Jamie slid on a pair of black slacks and glanced at his watch. Six-thirty. They would be meeting at Northern Oaks, an upscale restaurant a couple of blocks from his condo, at seven. He hurriedly finished getting dressed and made it out the door with twenty minutes to spare.

Jamie had reserved a table outside on the second-story, cast-iron balcony, which always reminded him of the French Quarter of New Orleans. The evening had cooled down, and he sought to take advantage of the nice weather. He was shown to their table and waited patiently for his dinner guests to arrive. He'd offered to pick them up but Carrie had insisted on meeting him there.

Jamie ordered four ice waters and a bottle of his favorite red wine while he waited. At seven on the dot, Carrie and her parents arrived. Carrie looked elegant in a white pantsuit and flesh-colored pumps. White was her favorite color and Jamie understood why—she was breathtaking in it. Her raven coils were brushed back into a low ponytail. She smiled when she saw him, and Jamie stood and kissed her on the cheek.

"Good evening, gorgeous."

"Good evening, handsome," she responded with a flirtatious grin.

Jamie bowed his head and politely kissed Mrs. King's hand. Debra was wearing a gold sequin evening gown, a little overdressed in Jamie's opinion, but not unlike her. She slightly nodded her head at Jamie, letting him know that she wasn't the least bit impressed, and took her seat. Mr. King gave him a firm handshake, and a friendly greeting. He was a bit more casual, dressed in a pale blue collared shirt and khakis.

Once they all were seated, Debra wasted no time being her normal pompous self.

"I hope the food is adequate," she said, staring at the menu. "I haven't had a decent meal since I've been in this town."

Jamie ignored her and leafed through the menu. She would not provoke a reaction from him tonight. He was determined to keep his peace.

"Dear," Richard King said, gently patting her hand, "we've had several good meals since we've been here. Lucille's was delicious, wasn't it?"

Debra gave her husband a cold stare. "Speak for yourself."

Richard's smile faded, and his focus returned to the menu. Once they ordered their meals, Jamie poured them all a glass of wine and said, "Let's make a toast."

"And what are we toasting to?" asked Debra.

"To a future filled with happiness and loving one another endlessly," Carrie interjected.

"Humph," Debra said but toasted anyway.

She grimaced after tasting the wine and placed the glass back on the table like she wanted nothing to do with it. "I'll never understand the fondness for sweet wine. It's abhorrent."

Jamie took a sip and smiled. The sweet red he'd ordered was one of his favorites, and he wasn't about to let her ruin his good thing.

"So, Jameson, what was all the commotion about during your and Carrie's engagement party?"

So she was determined to ruin at least one of his good things.

Jamie eyed Carrie who said, "Mother, Jamie and I have already resolved that matter. No need to address it further."

"Have you now? So, this Tiffany is no longer in the picture?"

"Her name is Teylor," Jamie corrected with a hint of irritation.

Carrie snapped her head around to face Jamie. He met her eyes without blinking. He knew what she was thinking—he was defending Teylor. Maybe he was; he couldn't be sure, but he *was* sure that Debra was racking his last nerve.

"I'll take that as a yes," Debra mumbled.

"Dear, please. Let's not make this a big deal," Richard cautioned. "You heard Carrie. They've resolved the matter. No need to linger on it."

Another sharp look from his wife, and Richard was quiet again. This time he took a hard gulp of his wine, and Jamie shook his head. He never understood how men could be so spineless. Clearly the man's wife was out of line, and Richard couldn't even bring himself to let her know. Jamie vowed he would never be like that. He also wondered if he'd be able to live with the two of them as his in-laws. Holidays with them would be tough.

"You know, Jameson, I've seen all kinds of people ruin marriages, friends included," Debra continued.

"Does that also include in-laws?" he retorted, taking another sip of wine.

Mrs. King's eyes widened in shock. A look of surprise settled on Carrie's face but she remained silent. Richard nursed his drink, too intimidated to get involved. Debra's mouth opened in retaliation, but before she could respond, the waiter returned with their entrees. Jamie felt relieved by the distraction. He was in no mood to enter into a war of words with her. In fact, he was on the brink of getting up and walking home. Whether Carrie would be offended or not no longer concerned him. He refused to let Debra continue to belittle him. He showed her respect, and he expected the same treatment in return.

The majority of their meal was eaten in silence with only Carrie and Richard making small talk here and there. Jamie and Debra remained quiet—unspoken tension lingered. Once she was ready, Mrs. King resumed her condescending ways.

"I can't wait to return to New York where the food is decent and the people are"—she glanced at Jamie—"dignified."

Jamie wanted to tell her that he'd have the airport shuttle waiting for her by the time she returned to the hotel but thought better of it.

"Mother, Spirit Lake isn't that bad."

Jamie eyed Carrie. "Not that bad? I thought you liked it here," he said, puzzled.

"I do. I mean…it's beautiful…I just think that New York is more my style. Or Paris."

Her confession reminded Jamie of what Teylor had said. Carrie was Paris; he was Spirit Lake. Did she think he was good enough for her? Or even more importantly, was she what he really wanted?

"Face it, Jameson, Carrie's not a small-town girl. She's classy and elegant. You can count on it; the two of you won't be living here much longer after you're married. Happy wife, happy life," Debra informed him.

Jamie meditated on her words. He hadn't agreed to move anywhere and wasn't sure he wanted to.

"We haven't really discussed any of this. My business is in Phoenix. My family is in Spirit Lake. I've been here my whole life," he said.

"Well, the same is true with her," Mrs. King countered. "You can't expect Carrie to live here forever." She threw her hands out, gesturing toward the town.

When Jamie looked at Carrie, she was quiet but her eyes agreed with her mother. Jamie chose to not speak further on the matter. He and Carrie would have to have a serious talk—just the two of them.

"Jameson, a woman like Carrie needs the finer things in life. I've raised her to appreciate them."

Jamie's curiosity piqued. "And what would these 'finer things' be?" He was asking Debra but looking at Carrie.

"Jamie," Carrie warned, but Jamie couldn't stop. He needed to know how much Carrie was like her mother.

"Maybe you could answer the question, love," Jamie said, staring intently at his fiancée.

"Nonsense," Debra intervened. "Just look at her. Does she look like a woman who would take up residence in this backwater?"

"Mother!" Carrie shouted.

"Well?" Mrs. King insisted.

"I'd like to know too," Jamie agreed.

Carrie made eye contact with Jamie. Her silence was deafening but revealing at the same time, and he no longer needed to hear an answer. The lack of one told him all he needed to know.

"Now let's wait a minute here," Mr. King said. "You two have all the time in the world to decide what will be right for your family. You don't need to have a definite answer right this minute."

"Richard."

"Oh hush, Debra," he said, waving a hand. "Marriage is hard enough without us sticking our noses in it and telling them what they should or should not do. We had to find our own way; let's let them find theirs."

Debra sat shell-shocked, but Jamie was glad the man had finally stood up for himself. Even Carrie looked pleasantly surprised that her father had finally used his voice.

Jamie raised his glass and said, "Cheers to that."

They all, aside from Debra, raised their glasses, but Jamie couldn't help but notice the reluctance and uncertainty on Carrie's face.

~

Teylor entered Rima's building through the side door. Her apartment was located above Songbird Café, and when the café was closed, the side entrance was the only way to access her apartment. She made her way up the staircase to the second floor. When Rima had suggested at the lake that they get together for girl time in the evening, Teylor had jumped on the invitation. She could use the company, and since Jamie was tied up, Rima was her closest friend.

Teylor knocked on the wooden yellow door. When Rima answered it, her smile was as bright as the multicolored sarong dress she was wearing. With her red locks tied into a high bun, she embraced Teylor and ushered her in.

"Finally we get to have a little girl time," she shouted as she walked into the kitchen.

"Tell me about it," Teylor responded. "I could use it."

Teylor made herself comfortable on Rima's red couch. She always loved coming to this apartment. As different as they were in style, Teylor had a genuine appreciation for Rima's taste. Her apartment was shrouded in every color and plant you could imagine. Red couch, yellow chairs, blue coffee table, purple drapes, an assortment of pillows containing all of the colors known to man, and soft green walls. Yet it all came together beautifully. Teylor always joked that she'd entered an island retreat when she stepped into Rima's place.

Rima came bouncing out of the kitchen with wineglasses and an open bottle of red wine. There was already a cheese and cracker tray sitting on the table. Rima poured the wine into their glasses, grabbed a slice of cheese, and sank back into one of the yellow chairs.

"Are you still feeling empowered after everything that happened last night?" she asked.

Teylor sighed and responded, "I'm so tired of talking about me and what's going on in my life. Let's talk about your drama for a change. What's going on with you?"

"Me?" Rima asked, her eyebrows raising to the sky.

"Yes, you. You do have a life, don't you?"

Rima shrugged carelessly. "I mean, yeah, but…nothing interesting besides the café. You don't really want to hear about that, do you?"

"Yes, actually I do. I thought your show was amazing last night. I hope you understand why I left when I did—nothing to do with you. How did everything go afterwards though? It was a great turnout."

"It was. I was happy with it. I received a lot of compliments on my voice—and I got a standing ovation at the end. Some people said they didn't know I had it in me."

Teylor smiled. She was so happy for Rima. She could see the excitement in her friend's eyes.

"There were a lot of people from out of town there last night."

Rima nodded. "Yeah, quite a few came from Phoenix. I met a guy who said he's a local producer. He wants to get me in the studio."

Teylor's eyes lit up. "You're kidding!"

"Nope. I'm supposed to meet with him sometime in the next couple of weeks."

Teylor jumped up from the couch and wrapped Rima in a hug. "That's awesome, Rima. Who knows where this could lead?"

"We'll see," she answered with a gracious smile.

Teylor popped a cracker in her mouth and sat back down on the couch. "So what else? Did you meet any potentials?"

Rima's faced scrunched up like a prune. "Girl, no. Potential what? I cannot be bothered with these guys."

Teylor's mouth fell open in laughter. "You haven't dated in a while. Are you just not interested anymore?"

Teylor saw Rima's countenance change. But when she noticed that Teylor was studying her, she perked up. Teylor considered whether or not to pry, but decided not to. If and when Rima was ready to talk, she would.

"I think I'm just wanting to focus on my music right now," she answered.

Teylor nodded. "Understandable. Love is too much trouble anyway."

"It isn't supposed to be, Teylor. We make it that way."

"Why do you think that is?"

"I don't know. Fear. Selfishness. It's probably a list of things, but one thing is certain, God doesn't intend for us to cause each other so much pain."

Rima was talking to Teylor but looking elsewhere. There was definitely something plaguing her mind.

"Yet we still find our way to it…pain, that is."

They both became silent. Teylor's thoughts wandered to her own dilemma, and Rima continued to stare at nothing in particular. Finally she snapped out of her daydreaming and said, "But He always brings us full circle. He always finishes His good work. Right?"

"That we can count on. I guess in the meantime, we just hang on and keep trusting."

"That's all we can do," Rima answered with a smile.

EIGHTEEN

I t was Thursday, two days before Jamie's wedding, and Teylor was at the bookstore filling in for Mr. Henry while he ran a couple of errands. The store was quiet with only a few people browsing or sitting at the tables. Teylor passed the time working on her novel. The day was cloudy, and though it looked like rain, it had yet to make an appearance. The weather made Teylor drowsy, but she fought to concentrate on getting at least a chapter done while she was there. She was so engrossed in her writing that she hadn't realized another customer had entered the store.

"Greetings, Teylor."

Teylor glanced up and to her surprise, Carrie stared back at her. For a moment, her words caught in her throat. *What is she doing here?*

"Uh...hi?" she stammered.

Carrie stood there with a smile on her face, her hair parted down the middle and tucked behind her ears. She still managed to look flawless in the jeans and white T-shirt she wore. Teylor was surprised she owned a pair of jeans, as sadity as she was.

"Is there something I can help you with? A book I can help you find?" Teylor managed to choke out.

"No, thank you," she responded politely. "Actually, I came to see you."

Teylor's brows drew together. "Really?"

"Yes, you see…I hate to sound impolite, but considering everything that has transpired, I think it would be in everyone's best interest if…let's see how can I word this? If you made other arrangements for Saturday."

Teylor was taken aback by her boldness. Her heart dropped to her stomach.

"Are you disinviting me to the wedding?" she asked.

"Well, that's rather harsh, wouldn't you say? Oh, who am I kidding? Think about it, Teylor. What would you do in my position?"

Teylor couldn't believe what she was hearing. The gall of this woman! Jamie was her best friend. She couldn't just miss the most important day of his life.

"That's the most important day of Jamie's life," she said, voicing her thoughts.

"The most important day of *OUR* lives," Carrie corrected.

Teylor looked away, her lips tight. Her heart rate increased by the second.

"So when you say 'everyone's best interest,' in reality, you mean yours," she said curtly.

"Does it matter *whose* best interest I'm referring to, Teylor? You brought this on yourself. Take some accountability and don't show up."

"He'll want his best friend there," Teylor snapped.

"Former best friend, Teylor. He'll get over it. I can assure you." With a wicked smile, she added, "Especially after the wedding festivities are over, and we're all alone in his bedroom."

Teylor wanted so badly to punch her in the face, but she'd been in prayer all morning and knew the Holy Spirit was keeping her temper in line. He was also keeping her from spilling her breakfast. She took a deep breath and calmed herself. She wasn't about to let Carrie see her fall apart like she had during their last encounter.

"I'll have to talk to him about it first," she finally said.

"No need. We've already spoken," Carrie responded, turning away.

She turned and faced Teylor again. "Just make yourself scarce…and let's be clear, whatever you and Jamie had is over."

Teylor held back tears as she watched Carrie exit the bookstore. She knew that things were coming to an end, but to hear it from Carrie was like a dagger through her heart.

~

Teylor was staring into space when Mr. Henry returned. News of the events at the engagement party had already made its way around town, so Mr. Henry had a good idea that whatever was bothering her had a great deal to do with Jamie's upcoming marriage, but the weary lines etched in her forehead spurred him to ask her anyway.

"Teylor," he said in his familiar friendly voice. He'd always reminded Teylor of what a grandfather should be like, but she'd never had the privilege of the real experience.

"Are you alright?" he asked.

She forced a smile, but refused to lie. "I've been better."

"Does this have anything to do with Jamie?"

She looked at him, still forcing the tears to remain confined. Her answer wasn't needed. He walked around the desk to embrace her.

"I know what it's like to lose someone you love dearly," he consoled her, gently rubbing her hair. "There were times I thought I might not make it."

Tears formed in his eyes as he remembered the pain he'd felt when Adel died. Mr. Henry moved Teylor away and met her glassy eyes.

"But for the grace of God…"

He waited a moment before continuing, his gaze focused and penetrating. "It's not too late for you, Teylor. Not while the both of you still have breath in your lungs."

A smile gathered on his lips. "You know, you two remind me a lot of me and my Adel. We were the best of friends before we realized that we were in love. Well, I always knew, but she needed some convincing," he recalled with a chuckle.

His eyes sparkled as he spoke of her, and his smile was endearing. Teylor admired his love for Adel and hoped to have someone speak of her in that way someday.

"I see you both at Lucy's every week..." His eyes traveled to a clock hanging on a nearby wall. "Right around this time," he finished.

Teylor dropped her eyes to the floor. "Yeah well, I don't think we'll be doing that anymore," she said barely above a whisper.

"Is that what he told you?"

She shook her head.

"Then how would you know?" he asked.

He had a gleam in his eye that encouraged her desire to see if he was right.

"Um, Mr. Henry—"

"I'm fine here," he interjected. "You go on."

She turned to leave and stopped herself, turning back to wrap him in a warm hug. "Thank you, Mr. Henry."

He chuckled and reciprocated.

"You get going now. Don't leave the man waiting."

~

Lucy's was moderately crowded with the same familiar faces, and Teylor waved as she glanced toward her and Jamie's table. Sadness washed over her to see it empty, but she decided to sit there and order anyway. Sandy came bopping over in her same checkered apron.

"Hey, T," she said excitedly.

Then she looked at Jamie's seat, and her mood changed. "Is he late?"

Teylor shrugged. She wanted to tell Sandy that she wasn't sure he was coming at all, but she wasn't up for discussing it.

"After what happened the last time, I'd be surprised if the Wicked Witch of the West allowed him to leave her lair," Sandy spat.

Teylor thought about her last visit to Lucy's, when Carrie had confronted her. As upset as she'd been that day, she really couldn't blame Carrie. After all, she'd probably react the same way if she was in her shoes.

"That's not really fair, Sandy. I mean what if some woman told you she was in love with your fiancé? How would you react?"

Sandy shrugged and answered, "I don't know, but what did she expect? She barely knows him and then insists they get married a week after she hits town. Meanwhile, you guys've been together for as long as I can remember. You were made for each other. A blind man can see that, and I bet she saw it too when she arrived. She's not mad because you're in love with her man; she's mad because her man is in love with you," she revealed with one hand on her hip.

"Anyway, I'll bring you some biscuits and sweet tea while you decide what else you're having."

Sandy walked away leaving Teylor to ponder her words. She'd never thought about it like that. Could Carrie think that Jamie was in love with her and that's why she felt so threatened? Carrie came across as sure of herself, almost overly confident. Surely, one woman wouldn't bother her, especially if what Carrie had said about Jamie seeing her as a sister was true. Teylor couldn't be sure, but it was definitely something to think about.

Teylor put her face in her hands.

This was all too much. She didn't even know how she'd ended up back in this situation. She'd been so sure she was ready to let him go, but if that was the case, then why was she sitting at *their* table waiting for someone who wasn't going to show?

"Hey."

The familiar voice pulled her from her thoughts and Teylor snapped her head up to face him. Her mouth fell open slightly when she saw him. Freshly cut hair and trimmed beard, smooth nut brown skin, clean crisp white T-shirt. His dark eyes pierced hers, and her breath caught in her throat. He was a beautiful answer to her prayer.

Jamie sat across from her, awaiting her response. When she finally found words, they came out shaky.

"I...I didn't think you were coming."

"I didn't think you would be here either," he answered. "Yet, here we are."

Their eyes held in silence. Sandy sauntered back over to their table, unable to hide her grin. She sat the biscuits and sweet tea down in front of Teylor and placed a strawberry lemonade before Jamie. He looked at Teylor.

"You weren't sure if I was coming, but still you ordered my drink?" he asked, holding up his glass.

"Nope," Sandy corrected. "I knew you'd show up so I brought it. Every week like clockwork, right?" she asked with a wink.

Jamie let off a dimpled smile. "Right."

Teylor couldn't fight her own smile. Words couldn't explain how good it felt to be in his presence again.

"I'll bring you your regular, Jamie. Oh, are fries okay today?"

Jamie nodded.

"What about you, Teylor?" she asked, looking at her.

"I'll have the same."

"Awesome. I'll put it in right away."

Sandy scurried back to the kitchen leaving Jamie and Teylor in silence. For a little while neither of them said a word. Teylor looked out of the window at the bookstore. She thought of Mr. Henry's words.

It's not too late for you, Teylor.

Teylor looked back at Jamie. He was watching her.

"Why did you come, Jamie?"

"Why did you?"

"I asked you first."

He chuckled at their elementary banter and then turned serious. Shrugging his shoulders, he said, "It's what we've always done. Things have been a little...chaotic lately. I dunno, maybe I wanted a sense of normalcy."

She was his *normal.*

At least that was the way she heard it, but why wouldn't she be? They'd been each other's *normal* for years.

"What about you?" he asked.

"I was just hoping you'd be here. I miss seeing you…in our *old* way. That's all."

"I thought you were letting go," he said boldly.

Their eyes held.

"Me too," she said quieter than she'd intended.

Sandy came bearing food. She hurriedly served them and rushed off to take the orders of the crowd that had suddenly gathered.

"Do you think we're still normal?" she asked, unable to meet his gaze. "After everything I said to you at the engagement party?"

Jamie stopped chewing the fry that he'd just popped into his mouth. He studied her and waited for her eyes to find his. When they did, he resumed eating, not saying anything. His silence made Teylor nervous, and she feared she might have just ruined their special meeting, but she couldn't go on ignoring the pink animal in the room. After eating a couple more fries, Jamie finally spoke.

"What do you think?" He asked it in way that said he wasn't trying to be sarcastic. He wanted to know her thoughts.

"I don't think things will ever go back like they were. Then again, I don't want them to."

His eyebrows drew together. "What do you mean?"

"I want a new normal," she said without hesitation.

He didn't respond, and Teylor decided not to press the issue. He knew what she meant by "a new normal."

"Where's Carrie?" Teylor recalled her earlier conversation with Carrie and silently prayed that she was nowhere near. She actually preferred her to be on the first thing smoking back to New York.

"On her way to Phoenix. She and her parents are finalizing some things for Saturday."

Teylor nodded slowly.

"And you?" she asked. "Are you ready for Saturday?"

Jamie glanced out of the window and back at her, taking a long pause. "Why didn't you ever tell me?"

"How could I, Jamie?"

"Easy. You say, 'Jamie, I'm in love with you,' like you did six days ago."

"And what would have happened then? The end of our friendship?"

"Really, Teylor? You know better than that."

"Yet, here we are."

"No, we're here because you decided to tell me a week before my wedding day instead of finding the time and courage to do it sometime within the last seventeen years. That's why we're here."

His tone was assertive, irritated.

Teylor didn't have a response for that. He was right. Her timing was awkward, true enough, but what's done was done—and to be fair, he hadn't given her much notice. Their relationship was on thin ice as it was, and she knew that once he and Carrie were married, it was over for the two of them, and she knew that he knew it too. Still he hadn't answered her question.

"Look, Jamie, I don't know what the future holds but I know that you're here for a reason…we both are. As much as I know it will hurt, I am prepared to walk away, if that's what you choose."

"If that's what I choose?" he asked, pointing at his chest.

"Yes, this is all on you now. I've done my part. You know how I feel."

"And you know that I'm getting married."

"Oh yeah," she stated with a hint of sarcasm. "The wedding you don't know if you're ready for."

"I never said that."

"Exactly. You never said anything."

Jamie inhaled and let the air escape slowly out of his nostrils.

"You know, Jamie, whatever we have or had or whatever, is about to be over. I don't know why you haven't addressed it yet, but I will."

She took a deep breath, building up the courage to say what she knew had to be said. "I'm forcing you to choose, Jamie."

His eyes narrowed but he kept quiet.

"Granted, you've already asked her to marry you, so one might think you've already chosen, but I don't believe you," she confessed, staring him hard in the eye. "You can't have us both, and we both understand that now. If you're going to marry her, then I wish you all the best, and I'll no longer be a part of your life. Period."

Teylor hated that she was being harsh, but she knew that she and Carrie could never occupy the same space in Jamie's life. Carrie despised her, and she wasn't exactly itching to be best friends forever with her either. Besides, if holding on to their friendship meant causing problems in Jamie's marriage and in his life, she'd rather not be a part of it. She loved him too much and only wanted happiness for him.

"You're telling me this two days before my wedding?"

She drew in a deep breath and straightened her back. "Yes. Yes, I am," she answered with no regrets. "I mean, you're so sure you want to be married, right? It has to be right now, right? So this should be an easy decision."

"For who?" he asked.

"For you."

"T, are you hearing yourself? Who wants to lose their best friend?"

"Is that all I am?" she asked boldly.

Jamie's words caught in his throat. Teylor saw the truth in his eyes; he was unable to conceal it, but still unable to allow his lips to reveal it. Unfazed, she stared him down, forcing him to answer. When he didn't, she reached into her satchel to pull out bills for their meal, but Jamie stopped her.

"No, it's on me. It's all on me."

NINETEEN

*J*amie's laugh pierced the night. It was her favorite sound. They swung on the porch swing—she sat upright and he was lying down with his head in her lap. They often spent innocent times like this together, sharing stories, making each other laugh. Teylor was telling him why she'd recently broken up with her boyfriend.

"I just couldn't get past his breath! It was something out of a horror movie," Teylor explained.

Jamie cried tears of laughter.

"Man," he choked out between chuckles. "You are so wrong for that."

"Nah, he was wrong for that breath," she countered.

More laughter poured out of him.

"Listen, when I get married, my man has to always have his breath on point. Otherwise, I'm going to start having some serious flashbacks."

Jamie roared.

"Seriously, Jamie."

She rubbed her fingers through his curls, and his laughter died down. Teylor could stay in this moment forever. He almost seemed to melt beneath her touch. His eyelids fluttered like they often did whenever she played in his hair, signaling *that he was close to sleep. She wasn't ready for him to drift off just yet, so she removed her hand.*

"Why'd you stop?" he asked, his voice low.

"Because you're falling asleep, and we haven't even watched our movie yet."

"No, I'm not."

"Liar."

A dimpled smile formed on his face as he confessed. "Okay, maybe I was. I'm awake now though," he assured her. He sat up to prove his point.

"I'm gonna have to get my wife to do that," he said, scratching his head.

Teylor smiled and asked, "What kind of woman do you want to marry, Jamie?"

"Haven't given it much thought," he admitted. He looked at her. "Hoping the Lord will choose for me, or at least let me know when she shows up."

Teylor nodded slowly.

"What about you?" he asked.

She sighed and looked out at the lake. The moon reflected off the water, and she realized how romantic it was being with him in this moment. She wanted to tell him that he'd make the perfect husband for her, but where would that leave them?

"I'm not sure either," she lied. "I don't know if I'll ever get married. I'm too picky," she said jokingly.

Jamie shook his head and grinned. "That's true. You're by far the pickiest woman I know, and I thought Charlie was bad. You've got her beat."

She playfully punched him in the arm.

"But seriously, T, you'll get married. You're too special not to make some man out there happy."

Their eyes held, and Teylor was glad it was dark outside so he wouldn't be able to see how crimson her cheeks had turned. If she had the courage, she'd have placed a soft kiss on his lips. Instead she said, "Thanks, Jamie."

She had to admit, she was picky, but not because there weren't a lot of good men out there. They just weren't him.

"Come on," he said, grabbing her hand. "Let's watch that movie."

~

Teylor sat on that same porch swing as the memories washed over her. Looking out into the night, she wondered if that evening would have been the perfect moment to confess her feelings for him. If she was so special, like he'd said she was, then why couldn't he love her the way she wanted him to? She'd given him an ultimatum at lunch earlier, but she was prepared to not be the chosen one. Regardless of the heartache, the Lord was her strength and like she'd stated so many times before, Jamie's happiness really was important to her. If he believed that Carrie could bring him more joy than she could, then Teylor hoped that was the case. She would never wish for his downfall.

The wedding was two days away, and she wasn't sure if Jamie was going to go through with it, but she was certain of one thing; she wouldn't stick around to find out. A change of scenery would do her good. Mr. Henry had several times mentioned a beach house that he and Adel owned just outside of San Diego. She needed to find out if his promises that she could use it whenever she wanted still held. If so, no one except for Mr. Henry would know where she'd gone, and she would swear him to secrecy. She needed at least two months to regroup and finish her novel, two months away from the distractions—away from Jamie.

With her mind made up, she headed inside to make the phone call.

Friday morning brought with it gray skies and light showers. Teylor floated face up in the lake as tiny droplets wet her face. Swimming alone in the rain was something she did whenever she got the chance, and today was perfect timing. After getting everything squared away with Mr. Henry last night, Teylor had booked her flight immediately. She'd stayed awake most of the night packing her bags and ensuring things would be okay in her home during her two-month absence. She'd be taking the unopened perishable food in her refrigerator to Ms. Lucy in a few hours. Instead of telling her that she was leaving, Teylor would tell her that it was a donation. Everything else, she'd throw away.

She didn't have to worry about her mail because the postman delivered it through a slot in her front door. She'd return home to a pile of unopened letters and flyers scattered on her living room floor, but she could manage that, as long as she didn't have to tell anyone where she was or explain why she'd gone. She wasn't completely inconsiderate, however. Mr. Henry would be sure to tell everyone that she was alive and well; she was just taking a much needed vacation and to please give her some space.

Teylor moved her arms in the water and thought about swimming in the ocean every morning—maybe the evenings too. The more she thought about it, the more excited she became. Waking up to ocean views and falling asleep to its liquid rhythm; riding Adel's old beach cruiser up and down the shore. Mr. Henry even kept an old Volkswagen van that he gave her permission to use whenever she needed. She'd write, exercise, maybe even take up yoga, try different dishes, and make a few friends. Suddenly, change didn't seem so frightening, and she was ready for the next journey.

The rain began to come down harder and faster, so Teylor flipped herself over and swam toward the dock. She climbed the short ladder and dried off with a large beach towel. As she looked up toward her back porch, she went still. Jamie was there, perched against the wall watching her. He wore a pale gray T-shirt that matched the sky and dark blue jeans. Was he there to tell her goodbye? She hesitated for a moment then remembered she had the strength to face whatever came her way, so she trudged on.

When she finally reached him, she saw concern that she'd been swimming in the rain, but he said nothing.

"Where did you come from?" Teylor asked him.

"Took the bridge over."

His voice was warm like always, but she could hear that there was something different in his tone.

"How long have you been here?"

"Not too long." He paused. "Saw you floating in the rain."

She looked away. Somehow she felt like he was invading her privacy. As if reading her thoughts, he said, "I didn't mean to intrude. At first I didn't know if you were okay."

"And then?" she asked.

"Then I saw you move."

She met his eyes again. "Why wouldn't I be okay?"

She thought he was implying that she'd harm herself. She might be going through a rough period, but that would never be an option. She had too much to live for.

"I didn't mean it like that. I just...we need to talk, Teylor."

Searching his eyes, she noticed that they held a hint of sadness and even though that scared the hell out of her, she slowly nodded in agreement and led the way into the house.

Inside, they sat on the pale teal sofa in the living room. Jamie admired a picture of the two of them as teenagers during a Fourth of July celebration at the lake. Teylor had her arm around his shoulders, and they were both smiling from ear to ear.

He smiled now.

"We had a good time that day," he said.

"It almost didn't happen," she responded.

He looked at her.

"My mom was passed out cold from one of her wine binges, and I told you I couldn't go because I was scared she'd choke on her own vomit and stop breathing in her sleep."

He stared at her intently but kept quiet.

"You knew how bad I wanted to go so you asked your mom to stay with mine so I could go to the lake. When I protested, you said, 'I won't have a good time if my best friend isn't by my side.' " She shrugged. "That was all I needed to hear."

They locked eyes for a short while. Finally, Teylor asked, "So what's up, Jamie? Have you reached a decision?"

He remained quiet.

"So tell me," she insisted.

"I don't even know what to say, Teylor."

"Just say whatever's on your mind."

He cast his eyes to the hardwood floor and then back at her.

"Are you here to say goodbye, Jamie?"

"Why now, Teylor?" he asked, ignoring her question. "I'm getting married tomorrow, and you expect me to cancel everything and just be with you?"

"I don't expect you to do anything. I asked you to make a decision. If you've made it, just tell me so we can both move on with our lives…whatever that may be."

She was angry. She already knew his answer so why was he prolonging the heartbreak? She wished he would just come out with it already so she could move forward.

"You know this isn't easy for me," he said.

"Easy for you?" she asked, raising her voice. "Do you think any of this has been easy for me? Hearing you tell me that you're going to marry another woman when you're all I've ever wanted? Seeing you parade your love for her all over town when I've been loving you for years? Do you understand how the possibility of losing you has almost destroyed me? It wasn't until I realized that I was losing you anyway that I got up the nerve to say something, and when I did, this is where we've ended up."

"Had you told me before, Teylor, you would have never lost me. You know that."

She let out a sarcastic laugh and shook her head in disbelief. "Then what do you call this? What happens now?"

A long pause ensued with their eyes locked.

"It doesn't matter now," he said quietly and stood.

Teylor arose from the couch and faced him. "What is that supposed to mean?" she asked.

"It means it doesn't matter anymore."

"It does matter. It still does matter. You mean everything to me." She placed her hand on her chest. "Don't I mean something to you?"

"You already know the answer to that."

"Then answer me, Jamie. What do I mean to you?"

"I can't do this with you, Teylor," he said, looking away.

"I'm in love with you. How many times do you want me to say it? How many times can I say it to make up for the times I didn't, huh? Do you want seventeen years' worth of I love yous?"

"I would like for you to stop saying it, actually."

She ignored his request. She wanted him to feel her soul with every word. "I. Am. In. Love. With. You."

"Stop saying that!" he yelled.

She jumped at his shouting. She felt her heart racing, and her eyes welled up with tears. Jamie threw up his hands in surrender, his countenance as defeated as the moment he'd found out his unborn baby had been aborted. That's what this moment reminded her of. All of the pain, agony, and despair that had accompanied that time in their lives had come back to revisit them, only this time, she wasn't his comforter. She was his pain.

"I can't do this anymore," he said through his own tears.

His chest heaved, as if he were struggling to breathe, like the very words that fell from his lips were killing him. She shook her head slowly in disbelief. If his words weren't killing him, they were definitely sucking the life out of her.

"Do what?" she asked, her voice trembling.

"I can't save you anymore! You have to live your own life! Walk out the plans God has for you! I can't take His place in your life anymore!"

"Jamie—"

"No, Teylor! You say this isn't easy for you? Everything I've ever done, I've always considered you first. The only way I would take over my father's company in Phoenix was if I could still live here to be with you! Because I didn't want to leave you! I drive back and forth three times a week just so I can live here! I've been feeling nothing but guilt since I told you I was engaged because I felt like I should have asked your permission first! I can't even enjoy my engagement, Teylor! Because somehow I feel like I'm destroying you and that's destroying me. When I proposed in front of the Eiffel Tower, all I could think about was if you'd approve. I. Can't. Do. This. Anymore!"

Teylor stood frozen in shock as water poured down her face in streams; breathing became more difficult.

Jamie wiped the tears from his eyes and said, "The night you recited your poem, you said that you were saying goodbye. This is me saying mine."

Jamie brushed past her and walked toward the front door.

"I'm leaving," she said abruptly, without turning to face him. She hadn't planned on telling anyone, but her hope was that he would change his mind if he knew that she wouldn't be around if he decided he'd made a mistake.

Jamie stilled, his hand on the door's knob. He'd heard her clearly but he didn't turn to face her either. They stood feet apart with their backs to each other, too afraid to witness the other's pain. Feeling it was enough.

"I leave tonight, and I'll be gone for a while." Her throat burned from the sobs she was swallowing. But she couldn't crumble now, not while he was still in her presence.

"I don't know when I'm coming back or if I ever will."

She paused.

"Ask me to stay, Jamie."

He was silent for a while, yet she could faintly hear his soft cries. Regardless of his decision, they were both losing their best friend, and she knew he was aching to his very core. She couldn't be the only one.

She waited, her breathing becoming shallow. Her head ached, and waves of nausea swept over her. And in one word her worst fear came true.

"Go," he said quietly and walked out the door while Teylor, upon hearing it shut behind him, crumpled to the floor.

TWENTY

La Jolla Beach was a satisfactory eighty degrees, with a mostly sunny sky and high humidity. Teylor sat on the patio that faced the ocean. She watched the waves wash upon the shore. Beachgoers lay stretched out on towels in the warm sand, hoping to get a few shades darker than their norm. Some rode the waves with surfboards, while others built sand castles or strolled along the coast.

She sipped her coffee and relished the sea air. Two weeks had gone by since she'd said farewell to Spirit Lake. The first few days had been hard. She'd even mustered up more tears she didn't know she had, but after being diligent in prayer and seeking God, after the first week, things started looking up. Soon the smiles came more frequently than the waterworks, and she owed all of it to the Lord. She knew she wouldn't have gotten this far without Him.

Teylor hadn't so much as turned her phone on since she'd landed. She checked only an email address that she used for work and refused to look at any of her social media accounts or watch television. She solely focused on quality time with God and getting through the different emotions she'd been dealing with.

A week after Teylor's arrival, Mr. Henry had sent a neighbor over to ensure that she'd made it safely and was doing okay. Deloris was a tiny, ginger-haired Asian lady with a round face and eccentric taste. When Teylor first opened the French doors to greet her, Deloris was wearing a jungle-print bikini with a yellow swimsuit cover that opened in the front. Every bit of her sixty-five-year-old skin proved her age, but she didn't seem to mind. She wore that bikini like a model walking the runway.

After spending some time talking to Deloris, Teylor discovered that her ancestry was Japanese, and she was a second-generation American, having been born and raised in Michigan. She'd been widowed for five years and in her words, enjoyed making the most of the time she had left. Hiking and painting were among her most favorite hobbies, but Teylor's eyes almost popped out of her head when Deloris mentioned that she'd recently taken up surfing.

"You only live once," she explained.

Overall, Teylor liked Deloris and enjoyed her company. She was two weeks into her summer vacation, and they agreed to get together for coffee at least once a week until Deloris returned to Michigan in early August.

A breeze flew by, and Teylor closed her eyes as she felt the wind blow across her face. She propped her feet up on the white rail that enclosed the patio and marinated in the moment, breathing in the salt air. La Jolla was turning out to be a good idea after all.

The house Mr. Henry owned was modest but comfortable. It was a two-bedroom, hippie-ish bungalow with pale green walls and colorful textiles spread throughout, which surprised Teylor because she never took Mr. Henry for a hippie. There was a small white kitchen and a decent-sized living room that led to the patio, which overlooked the ocean. On the patio was a hammock, a small table and chairs, and two lounge chairs.

The next morning, Teylor rose early to try out a small yoga studio nearby. She threw her curls in a high bun and pulled on a pair of black yoga pants and a sunflower tank. She'd decided on the seven o'clock hot yoga class, and by the time she was finished, Teylor was sweaty and relaxed. Back at home, she showered and ate a small breakfast consisting of grapefruit, eggs, and toast, then made her way back out on the patio to write. It was still early and the beach was empty. The only sounds were rushing waves and seabirds.

Three thousand words and three hours later, Teylor's stomach began to growl. She let her curls free and changed out of the sweats she'd thrown on and into a pair of cutoff jean shorts and a fitted white tank top. What she really wanted was Ms. Lucy's homemade buttered biscuits, but she would have to settle for something close by. The area was littered with various small chic eateries so she wasn't short of choices. She settled for Mexican and ordered Baja tacos and a strawberry lemonade.

As Teylor sat outside and ate, her thoughts traveled to Jamie. He was probably living in marital bliss, making love to Carrie and planning their next big trip to Paris. She forced herself to think of other things before she lost her appetite, but somehow her mind found him again. Was he happy? Was he thinking of her? They'd both eventually end up leaving Spirit Lake—him, because married life would pull him away to live in other cities, bigger cities; her, because what was Spirit Lake without him there? She'd probably never see Jamie again, and that reality made her eyes moist.

Nope, she coached herself, *you have to accept this. Life doesn't end here.*

Teylor finished the last of her tacos and lemonade. She didn't want to return to the cottage just yet. She wasn't ready to be alone with her thoughts. Instead, she checked out some of the boutiques and did some shopping. After a couple hours, Teylor started walking back to the beach house. There were so many tempting things she wanted to buy, but she decided to keep her spending to a minimum. With her future up in the air, she wasn't sure where she would need to be financially, so she only toted a small bag, which held a pair of sunglasses and sandals, home with her.

When Teylor reached the house, she walked around to the back door and found Deloris waiting for her. True to her style, she was wearing a hot pink, midriff-bearing top and jean cutoffs.

Teylor managed a smile.

After getting acquainted with Deloris for the past week, nothing surprised her anymore. A couple of days ago, Teylor had walked outside to find Deloris sunbathing on her own patio in the nude. When Deloris had spotted her, she'd waved as if she wasn't in broad daylight in her birthday suit. Teylor had waved back quickly and rushed back into the house. Later, Deloris apologized but insisted that Teylor get used to it if she was going to be hanging around for a while. Since that incident, Teylor made sure to look out the window before stepping out, just to make sure Deloris wasn't in a tanning mood.

"Hi, Deloris. To what do I owe the pleasure?"

Deloris grinned. "Hi, Teylor, dear. I was wondering if you wanted to have lunch with me today."

"Oh I'm sorry, Deloris. I'm just coming back from lunch."

Deloris's face dropped.

"Maybe tomorrow?" Teylor suggested.

"No, tomorrow is no good. I have a few procedures I'm getting done."

"I hope everything is okay?"

"Oh, I'm fine," Deloris answered, waving a hand at her. "It's just a little fine-tuning. You know, it takes a lot of work to look this good." She flirtatiously wiggled her hips, making Teylor laugh out loud. "How about a cup of coffee?"

"Ummmm, okay sure, Deloris. Give me...let's say twenty minutes to get situated and I'll be over."

"I'll be waiting," the older woman cooed as she sauntered off toward her condo.

As promised, Teylor was knocking on Deloris's door twenty minutes later. When she opened it, she'd changed into a skintight leopard-print dress.

"Welcome, dear, to my humble abode."

It was anything but humbling. Teylor walked into a gaudy, overly decorated den of furs, animal prints, and crystal. Deloris instructed her to have a seat on the purple sofa while she grabbed the coffee and treats. She returned carrying a gold tray with coffee mugs and cookies. She placed it on the coffee table and took a seat next to Teylor.

"How do you like my digs? I have to bring my own décor when I'm renting here. Otherwise, it's a dreadfully mundane experience. Everything is neutral," she finished, sticking out her tongue in disgust.

"I imagine the owner likes to keep things neutral to appeal to the different renters," Teylor explained.

Deloris fanned off the idea as ridiculous by waving a hand.

"I don't know how you take your coffee so I brought cream, sugar, and honey, just in case. My Sunny used to always take his with honey."

Teylor was silently thanking the Lord that Deloris had changed the subject. She couldn't bear to tell the sweet little lady that her taste was awful.

"Sunny?" Teylor asked with piqued interest.

"Oh, Sunny was my husband—a dreadfully annoying man, but I loved him more than anything."

She poured the honey into her cup and stirred. Her eyes held adoration and pain as she spoke of her late husband. "I've been coming here annually since he passed. It took me a while to get used to the sound of the waves washing against the shore at bedtime."

Teylor could relate. For the first few nights, she couldn't sleep for fear that the waves would come crashing into the house. The sound was now resounding.

"It must have been really hard for you, losing your husband," Teylor said.

Deloris softly touched Teylor's hand and smiled. "Still is. You never completely get over it. I mean, you spend forty years of your life with a man and suddenly...he's gone." Water glistened in Deloris's eyes yet she forced a smile. "But, you learn to live with it."

Teylor's heart ached for her. Here she was trying to cope with losing the man she loved to another woman, and Deloris had lost the love of her life to eternal rest after forty years together.

"But enough of that sad nonsense," Deloris insisted. "So tell me, is there a special man in your life?"

Teylor tensed for a moment, then forced herself to relax.

"Ahhhh, I see," Deloris said knowingly. "You know, body language will tell you an entire story without the person having to say a word."

Teylor sat her mug back on the tray. Her smile was sheepish, betraying her like her body had done moments ago. Deloris sat her mug down as well and turned serious.

"Your eyes look a lot like mine do when I'm thinking about my Sunny. It's hard to miss the sadness that lingers. So tell me, what's your story?"

Teylor took a deep breath. She was trying to heal and wasn't sure where rehashing would take her, yet Deloris sat there patiently with compassion in her heavily made-up eyes, waiting for Teylor to dish.

"Let me take a stab at it. You've had your heart broken by someone you love very much, and you're here trying to escape the pain."

"Pretty much," Teylor confirmed.

"And what's Mr. Heartbreaker's name?"

"Jamie."

Teylor went on to share with her everything that had transpired, from Jamie telling her that he was engaged to how she'd ended up in California. When she was done, Deloris was shaking her head and saying, "My, my, my."

"Tell me about it," Teylor responded, taking a sip of coffee.

"Deloris, do you think you will ever find love again?"

"Truthfully, I'm not interested. I've had the pleasure of knowing love that most people will never experience in their lifetimes. I lived it for forty years. I won't spend the rest of my life trying to match it, because I know that nothing will ever come close."

Teylor was moved but disappointed at the same time. That was her new biggest fear, that she would never be able to love a man the way she loved Jamie. She certainly didn't want to spend her entire life comparing every man she met to him. Seeing the defeated look in her eyes, Deloris placed her hand on her shoulder.

"That doesn't mean it will be like that for you, dear. Life has a way of surprising us. When the opportunity comes—and it will—go for it."

Teylor's eyes glistened. "How can you be so sure...that it will come?"

"Because everyone deserves a second chance, Teylor, even at love."

TWENTY-ONE

After her talk with Deloris, Teylor felt inspired to write. Over the next few days her book went from a few sketched-out chapters to having a full-blown outline. Teylor worked vigorously on her novel morning, noon, and night. She still met with Deloris every now and then for coffee, and the more they talked, the more Teylor wrote. She was fascinated with Deloris's stories about her trips all over the world, the interesting people she'd met, but mostly, the love she and Sunny had shared. Teylor seemed to be surrounded by beautiful love stories, yet her own was tragic.

The beach house exuded the love that Mr. Henry and Adel had shared. She could just picture the two of them taking romantic walks on the beach and sharing the hammock while watching the sun set. She remembered Mr. and Mrs. Westbrook slow dancing at the engagement party, staring lovingly into each other's eyes. And now Deloris spoke adoringly of her husband, who had hated that she dressed so provocatively but never missed an opportunity to hold her hand or kiss her in public. Even though Jamie had found love and Teylor wasn't sure she would ever love another man as much, she prayed that it would be different. She desired to have the type of relationship that transcended time. The type of love that only came with knowing God. The one thing that all these admirable couples had in common was that through it all, they never gave up on each other—but Jamie had given up on them. She promised herself that whenever God presented her with the opportunity to cherish someone again, she would never give up, no matter what transpired between them.

By mid-August, Teylor was in a good head space, typing the last words on the first draft of her novel. She had yet to come up with a title, but she was elated that she'd gotten this far. She decided to spend the next couple of days relaxing to celebrate. Deloris had already left for home two weeks prior, but Teylor still had another two weeks before she was due to return to Spirit Lake.

It was early evening, the sun hung low in the western sky, and Teylor lay in the hammock reading a book. The tides were strong, and she took pleasure in hearing the waves crash against the shore. When she laid her book on her chest and looked out to sea, from the corner of her eye, she glimpsed a figure standing on the patio of the house that Deloris had recently vacated. A more thorough look revealed a tall, shirtless dark-skinned man taking in the ocean views. Teylor hadn't realized that a new guest had rented the home.

She continued to stare, curiosity getting the best of her. The man wore black swim trunks and matching swim shoes. She could tell from the muscles lacing his back that he was in good shape. When he glanced her way, she quickly hid her face with the book she was reading.

"Dang it," she said aloud.

After waiting a few moments, she peeked over the top of the book to see if her new neighbor was still watching her, only to find that he'd vanished. Her eyes searched the beach, but he was nowhere to be found.

Maybe he went back inside.

Finally she saw his head come out of the water and dip back under. He rode the waves and swam with the tide. Teylor forced herself to get back to her book and stop being nosy, but somehow the book was no longer of interest to her. She saw the man come out of the water and head back toward the house. His eyes traveled to her again, then he took a detour and came her way.

"Oh my gosh," Teylor said, her heart racing.

She took a deep breath and played it cool, but when he got close enough for her to get an eyeful, the nerves crept back up. He was handsome. Extremely handsome. Dark skin, black eyes, long thick eyelashes, and a muscular physique. He was tall, maybe an inch or two taller than Jamie. Teylor guessed about six foot three or four. He walked to the foot of the patio steps and stalled, dripping salt water. His smile only added to his attractiveness.

"Hi," he said. "I'm your new neighbor for a couple of weeks. I'm Jordan. Jordan Johnson."

He ascended to the top of the steps and extended a hand. Teylor hesitantly got up from the hammock and shook it.

"I'm Teylor," she responded. "Nice to meet you."

"Pleasure's all mine," he said, smiling.

Teylor didn't reciprocate. She didn't know this man from Adam, and she wasn't sure what to expect.

"Are you related to Mr. Henry?"

"You know Mr. Henry?" Teylor asked, puzzled.

He nodded his head. "Since I was a boy."

Hooking a thumb toward the house he was occupying, he said, "A good friend of mine owns the house. His grandfather and Mr. Henry go way back. We used to come here when we were teenagers with my friend's grandparents and stay at Mr. Henry's place. My buddy loved it so much he decided to buy the place next door when Mr. Henry stopped renting, after Mrs. Henry died," he explained.

Teylor nodded but remained quiet, wondering where exactly he would have met Mr. Henry then.

"Have you heard of Anointed Faith Ministries in Phoenix? Well, the pastor is the good friend that I'm speaking of. That's his place."

Teylor raised an eyebrow. "Your friend is Bishop Morton Pierce?"

"So you do know the church."

"Everyone knows the church. It's one of the biggest churches in the country," she informed him.

"So it is. I'm co-pastor. Pastor Jordan Johnson."

Teylor gave him a skeptical look.

He chuckled. "I wouldn't lie. Google it."

Teylor took him up on his offer and googled the church's website on her iPad. A quick read of the website's "leaders" page, with a photo as more proof, confirmed Jordan's story. When Teylor looked at him again, he was grinning at her. He threw his hands up and said, "I'm harmless, really."

Teylor smiled, embarrassed. "I'm sorry, Pastor."

"Please, Teylor, call me Jordan."

"Jordan. I apologize."

"No worries. I don't blame you. Can't be too careful," he assured her with a charming smile.

"Well, to answer your question, no, I'm not related to Mr. Henry but I've also known him since I was little. We're from the same town in Arizona."

"So you're from Spirit Lake," he said as more of a statement than a question.

"Yes."

He nodded. "Beautiful town."

"Yes, it is."

"So are you just here for a little R and R?"

Teylor casually looked away. "I guess you can say that."

She met his eyes again. "What about you?"

"Pretty much. Just arrived today, and I have two weeks of relaxing ahead of me."

"Sounds nice. I know how hard pastors work, trying to meet the needs of the people. You guys deserve the time away."

"Thank you, but it's hardly work when you've been called to do it. It's very fulfilling."

"I'm sure, but still, everyone needs rest—even from the things they love."

"I can't argue with you there," he responded.

Their eyes held for a moment and all Teylor could think about was how gorgeous his were. There was definitely chemistry brewing between them, and the realization made Teylor look away.

"Well, I'll let you get back to your book," he said finally.

Teylor smiled warmly. "It was nice to meet you, Jordan."

"You as well, Teylor. I'll see you around."

Over the next couple of days, Teylor saw Jordan in passing. They exchanged casual hellos when he was on his way out or swimming in the ocean or Teylor was coming back from yoga. The night of their first meeting, she'd returned to the church's website to find out more information about the handsome pastor.

Anointed Faith ministries was a mega church located in Phoenix. Bishop Morton Pierce was the head pastor and the face of the church—and he also happened to be a very good-looking guy with a stunning wife who resembled an actress Teylor admired. She'd visited the church a couple of times but never had the pleasure of meeting any of the pastors. With a church of that size, she wasn't surprised that she hadn't known Jordan was the co-pastor. Mega churches were mostly run like businesses, church faculty were more like employees and members were clients. If she had been a member, she doubted that Jordan would even know.

Anointed Faith had been started by Bishop Pierce's grandfather years ago in his living room with five members, but didn't reach the level it was now until Morton became pastor. A fifty thousand square foot campus with mountain views housed an average of twenty thousand congregants weekly; it was the most popular church in the Phoenix metropolitan area.

Teylor shook her head at the numbers. She wasn't one to judge those who preferred them, but mega churches weren't her thing. She'd much rather enjoy the fellowship of the small church she was used to in Spirit Lake.

Pastor Jordan Johnson's bio described him as a former troublemaker who found God after several years of walking the wrong path. He and Morton Pierce had grown up together. And as neither had siblings, they were more like brothers than friends.

Teylor set her phone aside and thought of finding love again. She wasn't blind to the fact that she and Jordan were attracted to each other, but falling for such a public figure was not something she was interested in pursuing, then again, she was done planning her life. She was leaving it in the Lord's hands.

Teylor took advantage of the warm weather and jogged along the coast. She made it two miles before turning around and heading home. When she finally made it back, she kicked off her shoes and ran straight into the water. The salty bath was refreshing, washing away the sweat that she'd worked up jogging. Afterward, she saw Jordan standing over the grill on his patio. She waved and he called out to her. "Join me for lunch?"

Teylor thought about it before answering. She was fixed on saying no but then decided that she wouldn't mind having lunch with him. She was actually anxious to learn more about him, so she agreed to come over in half an hour.

She hurried to shower and wash her hair. She brushed her hair upward into a high bun, filled in her eyebrows, and smoothed a clear gloss on her lips. The humidity was much too high to tolerate any additional makeup. She slipped on a turquoise spaghetti-strap maxi dress and gold flip-flops, then made her way to Jordan's for lunch.

When she arrived on his patio, he was walking out of the house carrying a pitcher of ice-cold lemonade and two glasses. He halted upon seeing her. A smile dawned on his lips and said, "You look beautiful, Teylor."

She resisted smiling back, even though she wanted to, and responded with a calm, "Thank you."

"Please, have a seat anywhere you'd like," he instructed, setting the lemonade and glasses down on the table and hurrying back into the house.

A beat later, he was back out with a serving dish in one hand and a bowl filled with yellow rice in the other.

"I hope you're not allergic to seafood. I probably should have asked beforehand but I didn't think about it until after I'd invited you to join me."

"I'm not."

"So scallops are okay?" he asked.

"Scallops are perfect."

His smile was one of relief, and after grabbing one more dish, a summer salad, they were ready to sit down and eat. Everything looked delicious, and Teylor was happy that she'd chosen to come.

"Do you want to say grace or should I?"

Teylor froze. His words echoed Jamie's, and suddenly she wasn't sure she was ready to get to know anyone new just yet. Maybe she needed more time.

"Did I say something wrong?"

Concern was etched in his face, and Teylor realized how ridiculous she was being. Jamie could not consume her every waking moment. He wasn't the only person in the world who said grace. She forced a smile.

"No. I'm sorry." She laughed. "You can say grace."

"You sure, because if it's a problem—"

"No problem, Jordan. Please go ahead."

After saying grace, they piled their plates with the food.

"I can't believe you made all of this," Teylor said biting into a scallop.

"Why is that? Do I strike you as the type that can't cook?"

Teylor shrugged. "I don't know. I just haven't met that many men who can, I guess."

"Well, my father taught me well," he responded.

Teylor tossed a surprised look his way.

"Yes, my father," he repeated. "Don't get me wrong, my mother could cook, but my dad was a beast in the kitchen. Seafood was his specialty."

"Where are your parents now?"

"With the good Lord."

"Oh, I'm sorry to hear that."

"Don't be. It happened a long time ago. I've found peace with it."

Teylor kept her eyes down and forked some salad in her mouth. She was happy for Jordan, that he'd found peace, and was hoping that one day she'd feel the same about losing her mother. The healing process was slow, and some days she wasn't sure she'd make it, but she was progressing and for that, she was thankful.

Jordan must have seen the solemn look on her face because he asked her, "Are your parents with the Lord as well?"

She nodded. "My father passed before I was born, but it's only been two years for my mom."

She swallowed some lemonade to drown the lump forming in her throat.

"Give it time," Jordan advised. "Allow Jesus to finish the healing process in your heart and mind. It gets hard and sometimes you wonder if the pain will ever go away, but I promise you, if you let Him work, you will feel whole again."

Teylor was touched by his kind words and she gave him a genuine smile. "Thanks, Jordan.

"Let's talk about something a little lighter," she suggested then. "So, how long have you been a pastor?"

"Ten years."

"And what's it like being a pastor of a mega church?"

He stopped eating and looked at her. "Being a pastor is being a pastor, whether your congregation is big or small."

"Yeah, but there's a lot of exposure involved when a church gets to the size of yours. Isn't there a heavier weight on your shoulders to be what people expect you to be? More judgment?"

"I don't concern myself with people's judgment. I stay vertical." He pointed a finger to the sky. "People will make assumptions and pass judgments on you whether you're perfect or flawed. Only thing that matters is Christ. I mean, take Him for example; the most perfect being to ever walk the earth, and they still found fault in Him and sentenced Him to death. Who am I that I should expect to be treated any better?"

Jordan took a sip of lemonade and continued. "To be honest, the most difficult person I've had to deal with since I've been saved is myself. Killing this flesh every day has been the real battle. Trying to please my heavenly Father and not fulfill my own fleshy desires is enough of a weight to carry to where I don't even have time to pay attention to who's judging me."

Teylor nodded slowly. "That's very commendable. I feel like pastors have a heavier burden to bear, but it's good to hear that you're doing okay. I mean, it seems like your head is in the right place."

"Like He says, His yoke is easy and His burden is light. I truthfully can't take any credit. All glory goes to Him."

Silence invaded then, and Teylor stared out at the ocean. Sailboats seemed to stand still in the distance, giving the illusion that she was admiring a painting instead of real life. God's art was unmatched. Even the best artists could never re-create His glorious creation.

"So what about you?" Jordan asked, interrupting her thoughts.

Her eyes traveled back to his. "What do you mean?"

"I assume that you're Christian, right?" She nodded. "How did that happen? Were you raised in the church?"

Teylor's smile was uneasy. "No, I can't say that I was. My mom was...she wasn't really religious. A friend of mine introduced me to church and encouraged me to begin a heartfelt relationship with the Lord. He's been really instrumental in how far I've come in this walk."

"Is this friend...a boyfriend?"

Teylor's eyes narrowed. "I think I said a friend, didn't I?"

"You did. But your tone suggested otherwise."

His smile was knowing, and Teylor couldn't hide the flush in her cheeks. She dropped her eyes to her plate and played in the rice with her fork.

"Nope, he's just a friend. Nothing more, nothing less," she responded softly.

She could sense that he wanted to pry but he didn't. Teylor was counting her blessings.

"So, Teylor, are you single then?" His eyes were smiling when she looked up at him.

"Very much so," she answered.

She hesitated before asking her next question. "And you?"

"Very much so."

She opened and closed her mouth, deciding not to ask her next question, but he read her mind like a book and answered anyway.

"I'm thirty-eight."

She darted a quizzical look in his direction.

"You're pretty easy to read," he explained with a chuckle. "Your body language gives you away."

Teylor half smiled and shook her head. "I guess I always give myself away."

"Perhaps. It's not a bad thing, though. Most people who wear their emotions are not good liars, nor do they try to be. For example, you were being honest when you said that you were single, however, I can see that you're in love, and I'm assuming it's with your friend you mentioned earlier."

Teylor was rendered speechless by his spot-on assessment. His eyes watched her, waiting for a confirmation but she wouldn't give him one. Besides, her silence told him that he was correct in his assumption.

"You don't have to talk about it, Teylor."

"It's a long story, Jordan."

"Most love stories are, especially the ones that don't end the way we'd like them to. They're the hardest to talk about."

"Is it that obvious that my love story didn't end the way I wanted it to?"

"Your eyes are beautiful, but the pain behind them is evident."

"Yeah, well…" Her voice trailed off.

Here she was having lunch with a gorgeous man in a beautiful setting, but her heart wouldn't leave Spirit Lake.

"If it's of any consolation, he's foolish if he doesn't love you in return. Either that or he's too afraid to admit it."

She smiled and said, "You always know what to say. Occupational habit?"

"More like honesty. It's the only way to live."

"Okay then, Mr. Honest. Why are you still single?"

"Haven't found her yet, and just when I think I might've, I find out that her heart is already taken."

Their eyes held.

Teylor couldn't deny the truth in his words. Her heart *was* already taken, but meeting him gave her hope. Hope that when she was ready, she could fall in love again, and if he was to be anything like Pastor Jordan Johnson, it would be worth the heartbreak she'd had to experience to find him.

TWENTY-TWO

Teylor, with luggage in hand, stood on the patio silently saying her last goodbyes to La Jolla. Her time there had been replenishing, and she'd learned a lot about herself. She was even more grateful for the people she'd met—Deloris and Jordan, who had left the day before. She had exchanged contact information with both of them, but an occasional email wouldn't be the same as being neighbors on the beach. Most of all she would miss waking up to the ocean every morning, but knew she couldn't escape what awaited her back at home forever. It was time to tie up the loose ends and move on.

With one last glance, she inhaled the salty air and walked away.

~

Spirit Lake felt like a distant memory. Teylor's return brought with it memories of her last few days there. Some thorns still lingered but flowers had taken the place of others. She was healing. Being away had done her a world of good, even more than she'd initially thought it would, but staying away would have probably been even better.

Teylor drove through town passing all of the places she held dear to her heart. The beloved book store, Rima's café, and Ms. Lucy's diner. Leaving for good wouldn't be easy, but she'd make new memories and find new places to fall in love with.

Aside from the pile of mail scattered inside her front door, Teylor's cottage looked just the same as she'd left it two months prior. She brought back inside the plants she'd sat outside to get watered by the rain and placed them in their normal spots. She also wiped down the areas where dust had settled and lit some candles. Teylor wasn't sure how she'd managed to do it, but she'd had no contact with anyone from Spirit Lake the entire time she was gone. She still hadn't checked any social media accounts, and the only email account she'd looked at was the one she used for work.

Mr. Henry had given word through Deloris that he'd explained to everyone that she was fine but needed time to herself, and she hoped they understood. She contemplated calling Rima, but didn't feel like fielding the hundred and one questions she knew her friend would ask her, so she made a cup of tea and sat on the back porch instead.

California was alluring, still Teylor had to admit, she'd missed this view. The lake was quiet, but the birds weren't. Teylor didn't mind. Their chirping was nature's music. It always relaxed her. Soon she'd have to face everyone and provide answers and hear the town's news, but for now, she was thankful for this quiet moment.

She had taken an early morning flight back to Phoenix but wasn't able to sleep on the plane for all the nerves that were nipping at her. Swinging on the porch swing, sleep called her, so she stretched out and obliged.

When Teylor awakened, it was noon. Her stomach growled, and she really wanted to go into town for something to eat, but wasn't ready to let anyone know that she'd arrived. News traveled fast in small towns so it wouldn't be long before the people caught on regardless. She might as well enjoy what privacy she had left while she could. She settled for peanut butter and crackers.

Teylor sifted through the movies but couldn't decide. They all were movies she'd watched with Jamie so she opted to watch cable instead. By the time dinner came around, Teylor couldn't stand the thought of eating more peanut butter. She tried to think of an inconspicuous place in town where she could get some food, but that idea was next to impossible. She thought about starving until the morning. Maybe she'd be ready to face the crowd then, but her stomach wasn't having it. Ms. Lucy's biscuits or Connie's carrot cake sounded divine, but there was no way Teylor was going to risk running into Ms. Lucy or Rima just yet. She was about to give up hope when suddenly it dawned on her that the general store located fifteen minutes outside of Spirit Lake carried enough items to stock up for a few days, and no one from town would be there. It was her only choice.

Within thirty minutes, Teylor was pulling up outside of the small green store. She parked in the rear of the store to keep her car from view and checked her surroundings to make sure the coast was clear. Keeping with the theme, she wore a hat and sunglasses to keep from being recognized. Teylor made a dash for the store and once inside, took a quick glance around to make sure there were no surprises. When she saw that the small space was empty, she relaxed, grabbed a wire basket, and started loading it with goodies.

She was busy searching for beverages in the refrigerated section when the bell above the entrance sounded, alerting her that another customer had entered. Teylor stilled when she heard a familiar voice.

Rima.

Teylor ducked in the aisle, maneuvering away from where she heard Rima's voice.

What in the world is she doing here? She could have easily gone to the grocer in town.

Teylor was going to have to leave her groceries and get the heck out of there. Her eyes darted around in search of a rear entrance that she could sneak out of without being seen, but Rima's voice inched closer.

Who is she talking to?

"I can't keep doing this with you," she said. "All we do is sneak around. What is this? Just sex?"

Teylor almost choked on her spit when she heard Rima ask the question. She'd had no idea that Rima was even in a relationship, let alone having sex. She couldn't believe what she was hearing. *Who in the world is she talking to?*

Teylor let her curiosity get the best of her, and was about to peek her head over the shelf to get a good look, when the man spoke.

"You knew what this was when we started," he answered.

Teylor nearly fainted. She knew that voice. Saber. When had all this started? While she was gone? Rima and Saber supposedly couldn't stand the sight of each other, now they were being intimate? Teylor couldn't believe it. What else had transpired since she'd been away?

"But what are we now, Saber?" Rima asked, her voice filled with emotion.

Teylor was so intent on being quiet that she forgot to breathe. She slowly let out a breath, careful not to blow her cover. Saber remained silent.

"Fine. Then whatever this is, is over," Rima declared.

Teylor heard her heels clicking as she walked away, but the noise quickly stopped.

"Rima, I care about you. You know that. But I can't give you what you want. I never promised you anything more than what we agreed on at the beginning."

Teylor was horrified for Rima. She deserved better than what he was offering her, but Teylor had to wonder what Rima had been thinking when she'd decided to get involved with him in the first place. As long as she'd known Saber, he'd never been in a monogamous relationship—and Rima knew that. He'd always been extremely promiscuous. Teylor was rattled. Rima was so much smarter than this. How could she have gotten caught up this way?

"Of course you can't," Rima spat. "Go to hell, Saber."

More clicking heels sounded on the tile floor, then Teylor heard the bell above the door ring. Rima had gone. Teylor waited for Saber to follow suit. She heard him take a deep breath and after a few moments, the bell sounded again. The coast was clear. Teylor sighed with relief and stood upright. Aside from the cashier, the store was empty. She leaned against the shelf and tried to make sense of what she'd just heard.

Rima and Saber having an affair.

When did it start? Before Teylor had left or while she was gone? She recalled Rima looking sad when they were sitting on her porch swing months ago. Had Saber had anything to do with it? Did Jamie know? Saber had never been able to keep quiet about his conquests. Maybe the whole town knew, but then why keep sneaking around? Teylor looked at her basket full of groceries and decided that she'd better pay and vacate the premises before someone else decided to show up.

Back at home, Teylor stared at her cell phone. She wanted so badly to call Rima and check on her. Rima showed a tough exterior but Teylor knew she was hurting, and after her own recent heartbreak, she wanted to be there for her friend. Ultimately, Teylor decided to give her a little more time. Besides, Rima would want answers about Teylor's disappearance before she'd be able to get one word in about Saber. They'd talk in due time. For now, Teylor didn't want to think about any of it.

~

The next day, after speaking to a Realtor from Flagstaff, reality began to set in for Teylor. She was really doing it. Her home would go up for sale in a couple of weeks, and once it sold, she'd be leaving Spirit Lake for good. Per the Realtor, her cottage on the lake would be an easy sale. People were always looking for waterfront properties for second homes. Teylor had no idea, considering she'd been in Spirit Lake her entire life, but she took the woman's word for it. After all, when she had first laid eyes on the house, she'd wanted it more than anything. And now she was willing to say goodbye. Eventually she'd have to talk to her friends and tell them about her decision but she wasn't letting anyone stop her. She'd still see them regularly. Her plan was to move to Phoenix temporarily until she found where she wanted to be for a while. The cities and opportunities were endless, and she was ready to seize what she could of them. Maybe she'd even pop in at Anointed Faith and see a friend. The thought actually made Teylor smile.

Teylor grabbed a few empty boxes from the garage and began packing up some of the small items in her house. She didn't want to wait until the last minute and stress herself out. When she came to the picture of her and Jamie at the lake, her eyes misted. Before, she would have gone into full-blown sobs. The fact that she was able to control her emotions was a sign that she was on the mend. Teylor was grateful, but she still missed him. She didn't have the heart to pack it up just yet so she placed the frame back on the side table next to her couch and quickly walked away.

She snatched up her phone and went outside to sit on the porch swing. Without thinking twice, she fired it on and waited. When her home screen popped up, Teylor gasped. The green icon with the white speech balloon alerted her that she had over two hundred text messages. She was too afraid to check the voicemails. Teylor hesitantly pressed the text icon to see who the messages were from. Most were from Rima, of course. Ms. Lucy, Charleston, Sandy, Saber, and Mrs. Westbrook had all sent her text messages, probably wondering what was going on with her. The thought of reading them all overwhelmed her so she decided not to. Not yet. There were no texts from Jamie, but why would there be? He was somewhere out there living in holy matrimony.

She closed her eyes and breathed in the night air, forcing herself not to cry. After all that time, not even a text to check up on her. She was devastated.

Teylor stared out at the lake. For so long it had represented them, her and Jamie; their friendship. It always came back to the lake. Tonight, she wasn't sure what it symbolized. Deciding she'd had enough of watching it, she stood to go back into the house but paused when she heard the approaching sound of a motorboat. She looked to see who was coming but it was too dark to make out an image. When the sound ceased, she shook her head for so foolishly thinking that it could be him and turned to go back in the house. Before she could enter, her cell phone buzzed in her hand. Her heart nearly gave out when she read the text message:

Meet me in the middle.

Teylor's breathing quickened.

"It can't be him," she said aloud, turning to face the lake again.

This time, in the center, she saw a light flashing on and off. It was him. He'd done that before to alert her that he was there waiting for her. A slew of thoughts raced through her mind but she didn't have time to make sense of them. She scrambled to her boat and headed straight for the middle.

When she neared the other boat, she slowed, trying to make him out in the dark shadows. Realizing that she was unsure, he flicked the flashlight on, revealing his deep brown face. Teylor let out a sigh of relief and secret joy. She didn't want to get her hopes up, but seeing him again made her heart leap. She both hated and loved that he still had that effect on her.

She stopped her boat parallel to his and waited as he tied them together. When he was seated again, they just stared at each other for a moment. He spoke first, his voice pleasant and melodic, like a love song.

"How are you?"

Teylor's eyes were fixed on him, anxiously awaiting his explanation for bringing her there.

"I'm fine, Jamie. How are you?"

"I'm better."

"Better?"

"Yeah, better."

He kept his eyes on her while she forced herself to remain calm. So many emotions were invading her. Seeing him brought pure joy, slight anger, and faint sadness. Not knowing which would present itself, she decided to stay neutral and let him talk.

"When did you get back?"

"Yesterday morning."

"No one knows?"

"Well, you do, now. How did you know anyway?"

"I was sitting on the dock across the lake…saw your lights on."

Her response was a slow nod.

"So, how was your time away?"

He was making small talk, or maybe he really wanted to know. She wasn't sure, but she knew without a shadow of a doubt that he hadn't called her out here for a little conversation.

"It was good. Really good. Met some nice people."

She paused before asking her next question. "How was the wedding?"

His eyes dropped, and he stared at nothing in particular.

"So, you're selling your house?" he asked, avoiding her question.

"How do you know that?"

"Small-town talk, Teylor. You know how it goes."

"Indeed I do. That's why I called an out-of-town Realtor. Ummmm…yeah. There's nothing left for me here. It's time to move on, and I think I'm ready."

"Move on to where? Where will you go?"

"Phoenix first, maybe for six months or a year, and then, who knows. There are so many roads left to travel. I want to find my own."

Jamie's eyes moved away from hers and over the lake. He was quiet for so long that it scared her. Just when she was about to ask if he was okay, his next words stunned her.

"There was no wedding, Teylor."

Teylor sat frozen, all but her hands, which shook uncontrollably at her sides. She squeezed them into tight fists to tame them, but her insides were less willing to cooperate. She dared not speak, too afraid to ask him why. Too confused to be excited about the news he'd just revealed to her. Instead she waited.

Jamie sat quietly and watched her reaction. She knew he was reading her, and she knew he was waiting for her to ask. After what seemed like hours, her mouth fell open and she gathered the courage to ask what she desperately wanted to know.

"Why?"

His answer came immediately.

"She deserved better."

Teylor frowned and wondered to herself, *what could be better than him?* He was all she'd ever wanted.

Reading her thoughts, he said, "She deserves someone who will love her…the way that I love you."

TWENTY-THREE

Teylor's breath came out like a loud gush of wind; her eyes filled with tears. With her trembling hands she sought to free herself from him by untying the ropes that held their boats together.

"Teylor, what are you doing?" Jamie grabbed her hands, but she quickly snatched them away.

"Get away from me!" she shouted.

Jamie was stunned into silence.

Teylor pointed an angry finger at him. "You don't get to do this to me, Jamie! You don't get to play with my heart by deciding when you're in love with me! For years, I've waited to hear you say those words, and you choose now? After you left me to pick up the pieces of my broken heart? You almost ruined me, so no…you don't get to do this now."

Jamie stood in the boat and tried to embrace her. "Teylor, please."

Trying to break away from him, Teylor stumbled backward and fell into the water. Jamie jumped in after her and wrapped one arm around her waist, bringing her up for air. He held on to the rim of the boat with his free hand. Teylor squeezed her eyes shut, not wanting to look at him. Tears flowed effortlessly down her face. She felt as if her heart was breaking all over again.

"Jamie, please," she sobbed. "Don't do this to me. If you really love me, let me go."

"I can't, Teylor. I would do anything for you...anything except that. I'll never let you go, not again. I gave you space when you went to California. Mr. Henry told me where you were, but I didn't call you...I didn't text you. I gave you time. Time to heal from the hurt that I caused you. I know you haven't healed completely, but I can't stay away anymore. I feel incomplete without you. I love you.

"I'm so sorry for what I did, Teylor. If I could take it all back, I would. If I could take the pain you've endured and carry it myself, I would. Please," he pleaded. "Please forgive me. Be with me. I love you more than I love myself. You're my best friend, and I don't want to spend another day without you. Ten years on an island, Teylor. Ten years...a lifetime...I choose you. It was always you, and it will always be you."

Teylor's heart was overwhelmed. She couldn't believe what she was hearing. Opening her eyes to look at him through her tears, the sincerity in his eyes pleaded with her to believe him.

"I was too scared to admit that before. Too afraid to admit that you meant so much more to me than I allowed myself to see. I thought that maybe you needed me in the way that you need God, and maybe I was hindering your spiritual growth, but you leaving forced me to see that you've grown in a way that I hadn't realized. When you left, I felt empty. I won't let you leave again without you knowing how I feel. Even then, I'll follow you, Teylor." His eyes penetrated to her very soul. "I'm in love with you."

His words weakened her, and when he brought his lips to hers, whatever fight she had left in her evaporated. She gave in to his warmth, allowing it to erase the anger she harbored for him. Try as she might, she couldn't escape her truth. She loved him with every part of her being. The electric current that flowed through her body when his lips connected to hers for the first time convinced her fully.

When Jamie pulled away, their eyes met; and in that moment, years of friendship evolved into something much more.

Just for clarity, he asked her again, "Do you still love me, Teylor?"

"Yes," she whispered.

"Do you want to be with me?"

With tears still falling from her eyes, she answered, "Yes."

He smiled, those dimples she adored piercing his cheeks. Relief showed in his face. She caressed his cheek. It was hard to believe that they had come full circle. With another soft kiss, he said, "Let's get you out of this lake."

After docking the boats, they walked up the bank hand in hand. The nearly full moon bathed them in a midnight glow. For the first time in a while, Teylor's heart was full. The past few years had been more difficult than she ever could have imagined, and she'd often wondered when God would hear her cries and give her a break from the pain, but true to His Word, when she'd thought she could no longer bear it, He'd taken her load upon Himself, giving her beauty for ashes, the oil of joy for mourning, and the garment of praise for the spirit of heaviness. He'd pulled her closer to Himself, developing and nourishing their relationship during her darkest hours, showing her that He was all she needed, and when she'd finally accepted that revelation, He went above and beyond by giving her the man she'd loved since she was in the eighth grade.

Teylor gently squeezed Jamie's hand. "Do you want to stay over tonight?"

He gave her a skeptical look. "What did you have in mind?" he asked.

"Goonies."

Jamie chuckled and stopped her. Looking in her eyes, he kissed her softly on the lips.

"Absolutely."

THE END

ABOUT THE AUTHOR

I'd first like to thank the readers for giving Spirit Lake your time and attention. I hope you enjoyed reading about Jamie and Teylor as much as I enjoyed bringing their love story to life. This is the first installment of the Spirit Lake series. If I can be honest, in the beginning I wanted to shy away from making this novel into a series, but Rima, Saber, and Charleston were practically begging me from the pages to tell their story. I look forward to doing that and hope that you will follow along as we delve deeper into their lives. I would also like to point out that the town of Spirit Lake is a figment of my imagination. It was inspired by my love for small charming towns, and the true stories of freed men and women of color who traveled west to begin new lives and build their own towns after slavery was abolished. Writing my first novel has been an amazing journey and I am incredibly grateful. Lord willing, there will be so many more to come. Again, to the readers, thank you so much for your support. Lots of joy and happy reading!

I'd love to hear your thoughts. Let's Connect!

www.tamarriadenga.com
Email: TDwrites@tamarriadenga.com
Instagram: @TDwritespub
Twitter: @TamarriaD
Facebook: Tamarria Denga

DISCUSSION QUESTIONS

1. Who was your favorite character and why?

2. Given that Jamie and Carrie had known each other for only six months, why do you think that Jamie made the abrupt decision to propose?

3. Do you think that Jamie had always known that he was in love with Teylor, or do you think he realized it after she made her confession?

4. Do you think that Jamie made the right choice?

5. Did you sympathize with Carrie or Teylor? Why?

6. Who was your least favorite character? Why?

7. What was your favorite scene in the book?

8. Which place in the book would you like to visit most?

9. Do you think that Teylor made the right decision in being with Jamie, or should she have given Jordan a chance?

10. Overall, how did you like the book?